Fiery Fullback

The Chip Hilton Sports Series

For more information on
Coach Clair Bee and **Chip Hilton**
please visit us at
www.chiphilton.com

Chip Hilton Sports Series
#24

Fiery Fullback

Coach Clair Bee

Updated by
Randall and Cynthia Bee Farley

BROADMAN
&HOLMAN
PUBLISHERS

Nashville, Tennessee

© 2002 by Randall K. and Cynthia Bee Farley
Printed in the United States of America

0-8054-2395-8

Published by Broadman & Holman Publishers,
Nashville, Tennessee

Subject Heading: FOOTBALL—FICTION / YOUTH

1 2 3 4 5 6 7 8 9 10 06 05 04 03 02

GREG HANSEN

a Chip Hilton fan
and a friend of long standing

COACH CLAIR BEE, 1965

DAD,
Coach Clair Bee,
A promise fulfilled—

and to Chip Hilton fans
of all ages, of all generations

CINDY AND RANDY,
LUBBOCK, TEXAS 2002

Contents

**Foreword by
Cindy and Randy Farley**

FIERY FULLBACK

Foreword

DEAR READERS,

When I was a little girl, an absolute tomboy, I would watch from the doorway as my father wrote his Chip Hilton Sports series at my mother's dining room table. There was nothing I enjoyed more than watching Dad pound away at his old Underwood typewriter, a yellow number two pencil clenched tightly between his teeth, his white shirt sleeves rolled up to his elbows. Occasionally he would chuckle—no doubt at some of Soapy's shenanigans—and at other times he would mutter under his breath, and the white sheet of paper would come zinging off the typewriter to fall victim to a crushed fist and a disdainful fling to the floor. On such days, wads of paper like forgotten snowballs littered his feet. On more productive days, I would watch with glee as sheet after sheet piled high on the corner of the table. That was my cue. When the stack reached an inch or two, I knew I could pass by, grab the stack, and head out to my favorite tree looking out over the Catskill Mountains. There, safe in my favorite branch,

I would devour page after page of Chip's and his friends' latest exploits.

I loved those books. They were true and honest and so much a part of my Dad. I was sad when the books with the orange spines went out of print in the late 1960s. Little did I realize then that thirty years later my husband Randy and I would be charged with their stewardship and have the amazing opportunity—and honor—to share these great stories with new generations of readers. The updating has been such fun, and through his books, we feel we are keeping Dad and his great messages alive.

Dad lived during pre-Internet days, and although he received thousands of letters over the years from his readers, I know he did not have any idea of the degree to which his series had impacted readers' lives. Neither did we at the time. We are, in fact, just now starting to glimpse how dramatically vital the series had been and continues to be to so many readers. We are beginning to understand the role Chip and the Rock and the rest of the characters have played in shaping dreams, character, and lives for more than fifty years!

Not a day goes by that we do not hear from long-time Chip Hilton readers or brand new readers who write to express their feelings about Chip Hilton. Dad would be tickled, and we are absolutely honored to receive your E-mails and letters. Your messages are a tribute to Dad and an affirmation of the value of Chip Hilton in yesterday's, today's, and tomorrow's world.

Cindy and Randy Farley

CHAPTER 1

Always the Loner

WILLIAM "CHIP" HILTON placed the ball on the kicking tee and backed up until he reached his kick-off position on the lush green grass of Camp Sundown's practice field. The sun's late afternoon rays were beginning to etch long shadows across the field, elongating figures like a distortion mirror in a fun house.

Minutes ago Chip's team had received the opening kickoff of the intrasquad scrimmage and scored in just seven plays. Taking the ball on the five-yard line, Chip had sprinted straight up the middle of the wedge to the forty-one-yard line before Biff McCarthy adroitly decked him.

In the huddle, Chip had called for a double fake to his ball carriers and a delayed pass over the line to Chris "Monty" Montague, his tight end. The faking and timing had been precision perfect. Chip had first faked a handoff to his power back, Fireball Finley, who was driving into the line. Then, backing up and pumping his arm, Chip faked a pitchout to Speed Morris, who was cutting to the right.

Greg Hansen, the reserves' middle linebacker, had thoroughly fallen for the handoff. The bullheaded six-seven linebacker met Finley head-on at the line of scrimmage and was flattened and buried in the line. Montague had brush-blocked the defensive end and cut into the hole left by Hansen. Chip had flipped the ball to the six-three veteran, and Monty had bulled his way to the reserves' forty-eight-yard line for the first down.

When they huddled after the play, Finley had come in laughing and then muttered grimly, "*That* ought to teach him something!"

"Quiet!" Chip hissed. "No talking in the huddle."

Chip secretly agreed with Fireball's sentiments, but he wasn't about to express his thoughts out loud. For some mysterious reason and from the first day of training camp, Greg Hansen had displayed a strong animosity toward Finley. In the play, Chip had figured that Hansen would focus on Fireball because of his dislike for the big fullback. The call had paid off. From that point on, Chip kept the ball on the ground and alternated his running backs, Finley and Morris. They had carried the ball to the twenty-yard line in four plays. The reserves called for a time-out.

When play resumed, Chip faked a keeper around right end and handed the ball to Jackknife Jacobs, his flankerback. The reverse sweep carried to the four-yard line.

The reserves were stacked in a 6–3–2 defense, but Chip fed the ball to Finley. The hard-hitting fullback smashed through and over the line for the touchdown. Chip had successfully executed the point after, and now it was the reserves' turn to show what they could do with the ball.

Coach Curly Ralston was talking to the receiving team as they huddled around him near the bench. Chip seized the opportunity to look over his kickoff teammates. Seven of the offensive unit regulars who had started with him in last year's conference championship game were lined up along the thirty-five-yard line. The other three players were second-string veterans. Gone were flankerback Ace Gibbons, pullout guard Mike Ryan, and split end Red Schwartz. All three had played their hearts out in their last college game. The one-point defeat by A & M had been a heartbreaker for everyone, Chip reflected. *If only . . .*

Chip shook his head and growled to himself. *"Stop looking over your shoulder!"*

With his mind cleared, he focused his attention on the huddle. Head Coach Curly Ralston was upset because the offensive team had scored so easily against the reserves. Chip figured the coach was really laying it on the line inside that circle of players. It was no secret to anyone in training camp that Ralston and the entire coaching staff were concerned about State University's defensive weakness.

There was a shortage of offensive unit reserves, but no team ever made it big without a strong, rugged defense. All of Ralston's defensive units at State had been just that! For the past three weeks, the entire staff had concentrated on group work, with defensive play getting most of the attention. The coach had seemed to be satisfied with the offense, but he was far from pleased with the defense. There would be only one more scrimmage at Camp Sunrise after today. That game was scheduled for Saturday, only three days away.

It wasn't all bad, Chip concluded. Several sophomores and at least four junior college grads had distinguished themselves from the start. The junior college players were the most outstanding. They had held starting berths on an undefeated team for two years. Greg Hansen was a fullback, Whip Ward was a quarterback, Flash Hazzard was an end, and Russ Riley played center. And they were good! Good enough to make most Division One college teams, Chip reflected.

Chip shifted his attention to Hansen. The big junior college fullback was six feet, seven inches in height, weighed around 230 pounds, and was fleet of foot. He had declared repeatedly that he was a fullback and even announced that he had no interest in trying out for any other position. However, Hansen's tackling was so devastating that Coach Ralston had been using him as the middle linebacker on defense. "That's where he belongs," Chip commented aloud. "Even though he doesn't like it."

The tall newcomer grumbled, but he performed with savage aggressiveness in any position that Ralston placed him. But, as a power ball carrier, he wasn't in Finley's class. Not even close. Fireball had averaged six yards per carry the previous year against some of the best defensive lines in the country, and he was flawless in his execution of the plays. The big bruiser possessed uncanny deception in concealing the ball and was relentless in his use of precision and power.

Coach Ralston's line-blocking technique differed from that of most coaches. Instead of trying to force opposing linemen back through brute force, the strategy was to use their charges as levers to slant them aside. This style of blocking meant that a given hole in the line could change in a split second. Fireball was particularly adept at sensing line-opening changes and could swerve and hit in a new direction with lightning speed.

The blockbuster was a master of the sweep too. He could turn the corner and make the long getaway run.

Once in the open he was away with the speed of a sprinter. On the draw play, the play that kept opposing linemen and linebackers honest, Fireball had the speed and power to run right over and through them. Fireball's power thrusts had helped Chip's passing game, and he wasn't about to forget it.

There was a lot more. Fireball's memory could photograph opponents' defensive formations and changes even when he was blocking, faking, or carrying the ball. And when he came back to the huddle, he could tell the quarterback what play should work and what passing pattern seemed most likely to be effective.

Ralston released the receiving team at that moment, and the players trotted out to their positions in the receiving alignment. The referee blasted his whistle, and Chip lifted his arm and checked his teammates. They were ready. He moved slowly forward and tried to kick a hole in the ball. It was a high kick, and the ball seemed to hover lazily in the bright blue sky like a hummingbird coming at a feeder. Chip grinned in satisfaction. This kind of a boot didn't have to be a long one. It gave his teammates plenty of time to get downfield and tackle the receiver.

Chip was assigned to safety duty on the kickoff, and he slowed down so he could back up the waves of tacklers. Concentrating on the receiver, he saw a gap in the receiving team's blocking formation right where Hansen belonged. The tall newcomer had sped back past the restraining line, but, instead of continuing to his position in the wedge, he had turned and was now heading diagonally across the field—straight toward Fireball Finley.

Only ten yards separated Hansen and Finley now, and an old science question flashed through Chip's mind: *What happens when an irresistible force meets an immovable object? This* he had to see!

Fireball was moving with the speed of a gazelle on the open Serengeti Plain, gathering momentum with every stride. Chip glanced at Hansen and then back toward Fireball. He looked just in time to catch the big running back's move. It was a beauty, a perfect example of the veteran's deceptive running ability. Just as Hansen drove in for the block, Fireball changed direction and shifted his legs away from the blocker's shoulders. Simultaneously, without the loss of a single stride, Finley grasped Hansen's arms and, using the diving player's momentum, sent him spinning to the left and off his feet. Hansen sprawled on his hands and knees, and Fireball continued on toward the ball carrier.

Fearing the worst, Chip glanced apprehensively toward Coach Ralston. But the coach was concentrating on the ball carrier, and Chip breathed a sigh of relief. Hansen had deliberately disregarded his blocking assignment to get at Fireball. Only then did Chip permit himself a grin of satisfaction. If the sullen fullback had not recognized Finley's greatness before, this little episode certainly gave him something to think about.

Fireball's driving momentum carried him through the wave of blockers, and he met Aker with a crash that could be heard all over the field. The ball flew out of Aker's arms and bounded on the ground. Biggie Cohen took care of that! He gathered the ball in and sprinted across the goal line. Aker remained down, and Coach Ralston hurried out on the field with Murph Kelly, State's head trainer, trotting along beside him.

During the time-out, Chip continued his thoughts. Hansen had refused to accept the fact that Fireball Finley was one of the best running backs in the country. Besides, Mr. Indestructible liked to play every minute of every game. At six feet even, Fireball was seven inches shorter than Hansen, but he was just as heavy.

Fireball had a quick start and a tremendous second effort that enabled him to pick up two or three yards when his forward progress seemed checked. The previous year, Coach Ralston had used him both ways: as the power running back on the offensive team and as a cornerback with the defensive unit.

Chip noted that Aker was on his feet now, walking it off. Murph Kelly nodded to Coach Ralston. "He's all right, Coach. Just shaken up a bit."

"There's going to be more shaking up if we don't get some blocking and tackling," Ralston snapped. "All right," he barked, "let's go!" He turned away and strode briskly toward the sideline.

The defensive team huddled briefly two yards in front of the ball and then formed on the line of scrimmage in a tight 6–3–2. Ten yards behind the ball, Chip kneeled in the huddle and called for the placekick. "On three," he said. "Use good blocking now."

His teammates broke to the line with Finley and Jacobs positioned a yard behind the ends and Speed Morris kneeling six yards behind the ball. Speed indicated a spot on the ground, and Chip moved two steps behind that spot, lining it up with the center of the crossbar. Soapy Smith was covering the ball, and when Chip called his, "Set! Hut! Hut!" the ball spun swiftly and accurately back into Speed's hands.

Chip focused his eyes on an imaginary spot on the ball as Speed grounded it and then punched his leg through with the rhythmic swing and locked-knee action that had made him an accurate placekicker. The ball went spinning up from Speed's fingertips and straight for the center of the uprights. Chip kept his head down as he followed through on the kick, but he was aware of a charging figure that came hurtling through the center of the line. Still concentrating on the kick, Chip sensed that the breakthrough lineman was Hansen.

He followed the flight of the ball up into the slanting rays of the late summer sun, and at that precise instant the flying linebacker vaulted Speed and crashed into Chip with the devastating force of a charging bull. Caught completely off balance at the end of his follow-through, Chip was helpless. Hansen's vicious onslaught knocked Chip to the ground, whiplashing his head back against the turf.

For a moment he was stunned. He struggled uncertainly to his feet, fighting the daze that clouded his thinking. The running track that circled the field, the players, the bleachers, the goal posts, the camp buildings, and the elm-lined lake whirled and whirled around him as if they were fixtures on a spinning merry-go-round.

Bracing his legs to keep from falling, Chip fought the dizziness that fogged his mind and churned his stomach. Slowly, as through a cloud of smoke, Fireball Finley and Greg Hansen came into focus. Chip realized then they were slugging away at each other. He struggled toward them and was at the point of falling when Murph Kelly and Dr. Mike Terring grasped his arms. "Hold up, Chip," the trainer said. "Coach will handle it."

"Right!" Terring echoed. "Here. Sit down and sniff this until your head clears."

Lowering himself to the ground, Chip sniffed at the ammonia cap Terring had thrust in his hand. At that moment, Curly Ralston rushed between the swinging players. Grasping each by the front of his shirt, the coach pushed them apart.

"Break it up!" he shouted angrily. "What is this? A training camp for prizefighters or football players?"

State's head coach was nearing fifty years of age, but his tall, angular body was as solid as an iron bar. Holding the furious fullbacks apart, the coach glared at each of them in turn. "This has been coming on for some time," he continued, shoving them farther apart. "And I don't like it! No more fighting on this field by anyone."

He pointed a finger at Hansen. "You play football and forget fighting. Understand?"

"Finley started it," Hansen said angrily. "He hit me first."

"Finley may have hit you first," Ralston said sharply, "but *you* took Hilton out *after* he had kicked the ball. *You* had plenty of time to swerve aside. *That's what started it.* I don't go for that kind of football. We teach hard-nose football, or try to, but we don't teach dirty football or poor sportsmanship."

Ralston paused and took a deep breath. After a moment he continued. "You're a good football player, Hansen. Perhaps a great one. But you are also a stranger to us and to the kind of sportsmanship we expect from our players. Do you understand what I mean?"

Hansen nodded. "Yes, sir," he said. "I understand."

Ralston's face was still red from anger, but it was obvious now that he had his emotions under control. He whirled suddenly and frowned down at Chip. "Are you all right?" he asked.

"Yes, sir," Chip nodded. "I'm fine." He still felt light-headed but was sure he could shake it off.

"You don't *look* fine," Ralston countered. "Take him in and have a look-see, Doc." Turning to the waiting players, the coach gestured toward the track. "Five laps and in!"

Soapy Smith, Biggie Cohen, and Speed Morris, Chip's hometown pals from Valley Falls, hurried forward, their faces grim with concern as Dr. Mike

Terring helped Chip to his feet. Soapy picked up Chip's headgear, and the three regulars surrounded him for a moment. Before they could say anything, Chip reassured them. "I'm all right. I'll see you guys later."

"Not if he gets you inside that isolation ward of his," Soapy warned, glancing covertly at Terring. "No visitors at any time, remember?"

"Beat it, Smith!" Terring said shortly, rolling his eyes at the brazen redhead.

Chip's friends tossed their helmets on the ground in front of the bench and started around the track. Fireball was far in the lead, his shoulders hunched forward, his head down, and arms swinging, he was the picture of frustrated anger. Greg Hansen was far in the rear of everyone, circling the track with short, digging steps. "Always the loner," Chip whispered to himself.

CHAPTER 2

Fullback Mania

"LET'S GO, CHIP." Dr. Terring nodded his head in the direction of the infirmary. He led the way and Chip followed. As he walked along behind the team physician, Chip was thinking that the rivalry for positions hadn't been restricted to Hansen and Finley. There was a serious shortage of experienced players in most of the defensive positions, but, ironically, the outstanding challengers were competing for offensive jobs that had been held by veterans the previous year. "Including the offensive quarterback spot," he reminded himself wryly under his breath.

Winning a starting job on the varsity was the chief reason for a training camp, and hustle and hard play were directed toward that goal. But, he reflected, when competition fosters anger and personal enmities, it can only mean disaster.

Terring interrupted Chip's thoughts. "Hansen could have sidelined you for the entire season with that stunt," he commented over his shoulder. "What's wrong with that boy?"

"He wants to play fullback, Doc. He thinks Coach isn't giving him a chance."

"Play fullback? Replace Finley? He must be crazy."

"He can't compare with Fireball, but he isn't *that* bad. I wish he wasn't so hard to know."

"Someone *better* get to know him! He commits mayhem every time you players knock heads."

Chip didn't say anything, but he agreed with Terring. Greg Hansen's vicious play had been the cause of several injuries to other players. Chip couldn't call it anything else. Hitting a passer after he had released the ball was bad enough, but roughing the kicker was worse. Chip Hilton had been lucky.

"What are you muttering about?" Terring asked. "Does your head hurt that much?"

"My head is all right, Doc. I was talking to myself."

"An all-American quarterback shouldn't find it necessary to talk to himself."

"Thinking out loud is more like it."

"There's no question in my mind whom you were thinking about. Forget Hansen, Chip. Ralston ought to ship him out."

"Coach can't afford to do that, Doc. He can't afford to cut *anyone*. We're thin. Real thin. We have only three men back from last year's defensive team. Hansen can help a lot. He's a natural middle linebacker."

"He's tough enough," Terring agreed shortly.

"He sure is! Besides, middle linebacker is our weakest defensive spot. Hansen is fast for a big man, and his height would be a big asset in making pass saves and interceptions. Especially when the opponents have third down and long yardage."

Chip reflected a moment and then added hopefully, "Don't worry. Coach will shape him up."

"Personally, I don't think anyone can shape him up," Terring said. "An athlete who can't control his emotions and actions shouldn't be allowed to play *any* sport."

"But, football is his whole life."

"There's more to life than football."

Chip agreed with that sentiment. Hansen certainly did not. Off the field, the loner never talked about anything but football. That is, Chip mused, when he talked to anyone. About the only time he talked at all was when he criticized another player for making a mistake. His attitude had made him extremely unpopular with almost everyone. The exceptions were his three junior-college pals. Even though Hansen was disliked, Chip had noticed that the newcomers and challengers on the squad all turned to the loner for leadership on the field.

His thoughts turned to the team. This was Wednesday, August 22. A full-dress camp breakup game was all set for Saturday. The squad would depart for the town of University, the site of State University, on Sunday. Classes would begin the next day. It had been a disappointing training camp, he reflected. So far, there had been little evidence of team spirit.

To Chip, a school team was something unto itself—something wholly apart and different from a pickup team. A sense of unity pervaded that no real athlete would dream of breaching. Every player was an essential part of the team and bound by a spirit of loyalty to one another. This loyalty was the keystone of belonging and the trademark of a good team. No one said it straight out, but when one of the guys kidded another player with hard-biting digs, or gave him a little sideways glance of approval, well, then a player knew he belonged.

His hometown pals—Soapy, Biggie, and Speed—and the other veterans—chiefly Fireball, Eddie Anderson, Joe Maxim, Junior Roberts, Eddie Aker,

Jackknife Jacobs, and Francis "Biff" McCarthy—had team spirit. They had played together and valued the team. The junior-college grads, especially Greg Hansen, seemed too self-centered to grasp this important aspect of team play.

There was one thing Chip couldn't figure out. Why would the fullback position be so important to Hansen? Most candidates for a college team would have been happy just to make the squad; most would be willing to play any position. There had to be something significant behind Hansen's attitude. Why, Hansen hadn't even known Fireball Finley before camp opened. Chip agreed with most of Doc Terring's observations, but he couldn't help thinking how great it would be to have Hansen and Finley working side by side as teammates, rather than rivals.

When they reached the infirmary, Terring led the way into the examination room. "Hop up on the table, Chip, and let's have a look."

Chip lifted himself up on the table, and Terring's probing fingers gently searched the back of Chip's head and neck. "You landed hard," he said, "but everything seems all right."

"Thanks, Doc," Chip said, leaping from the table. "I—"

"Whoa! Hold everything, old boy," Terring smiled, putting out a hand to stop Chip's departure. "We still have to take an X ray."

"Oh, come on, Doc. It's nothing. I feel great now."

A faint smile swept across Terring's lips. "You want to take over my job?"

"No, sir. I didn't mean it that way," Chip grinned.

"I know you didn't. Let's get it over with."

Terring pressed the intercom button on his desk, and seconds later Sandra Ruiz, his assistant, opened the door. Ruiz's eyes widened as they shifted from

Terring to Chip and back to her superior. "Yes, Mike," she said, "do you need me?"

Terring flipped a thumb in Chip's direction. "Hilton got dumped a little too hard and landed on the back of his head. I think we ought to take a picture."

"Of course," Ruiz said quickly. "Ready, Chip?"

Ruiz took the x-ray expertly, and Chip sank down on a chair just outside the darkroom afterward. "Not now," he said half aloud, "not when everything is just beginning."

Fifteen long minutes later the physician's assistant came slowly through the darkroom door holding the photo between her two hands. She placed the film above the frosted top of the reflector and turned on the light. "Ask Doc to come in, Chip," she called.

Chip was reaching for the knob when the door swung open and Terring strode through the opening. Without a glance at Chip, he walked to the reflector table. Chip followed and stood beside Sandra Ruiz while Terring studied the lighted photograph.

After what seemed like an eternity, Terring turned to Chip. "I never realized you were so hardheaded," he said, tapping the frosted glass of the reflector. "We drew a blank."

"Thank goodness," Sandra said fervently.

Chip's heart leaped. He pivoted toward the door, but Terring's voice checked him. "We're not through yet, Chip."

"But you said—"

Again, Terring lifted a hand. "Hold it. I know what I said. Just the same, we're keeping you here in the infirmary for the night. Now you beat it over to the gym and get out of that uniform. Then you come right back. Understand?"

"But we have a strategy session tonight, and Coach will be going over the plays and picking the teams for the breakup game and—"

"And you will be right here in the infirmary," Terring added firmly. "As far as the plays are concerned, the Chip Hilton I know can recite them forward and backward. Besides, he knows he's State's starting quarterback whenever he's fit to play. Now you run along and do as I say."

"How long are you going to keep me in here?"

"Tonight and tomorrow morning for sure. If you are all right tomorrow afternoon, with no aftereffects and no temperature, I may let you loosen up a bit. Then, if you check out OK after practice, I'll give you a clean bill of health. All right?"

Chip nodded reluctantly and turned away. At the door, his hand on the knob, he looked back. The two were again studying the X ray. "Thanks," he said. "I'll be right back."

He walked out of the room and through the outer office. He realized Doc was right. He was still a little dizzy, so he took the porch steps slowly and carefully. Then he walked along the side of the infirmary and headed toward the camp gym. Just as he reached the entrance to the building, the door swung open and Hansen, stooping a bit to clear the opening, stopped short in surprise.

Chip was six-four but felt dwarfed by the towering fullback's height. "I'm sorry you and Fireball had trouble because of me," he said, blocking the door.

"Trouble?" Hansen repeated. "That was just the beginning. Finley hasn't seen anything yet."

"But why Fireball?" Chip asked. "I don't understand."

"You don't have to understand. It's got nothing to do with you. Anyway, I hope you're all right and I'm sorry I ran into you this afternoon. I lost my head. I've got nothing against you." Hansen stepped swiftly around Chip and continued down the gravel path.

Chip watched the tall fullback stride away, the rocky path crunching under his heavy feet. Then, still thinking about the big player, Chip entered the building, hung up his gear in the drying room, took a shower, and then walked back to the infirmary. Despite the rebuffs he had received from the sullen newcomer, he wasn't giving up on him. If Chip Hilton was going to back away every time he ran up against a tough situation, he didn't deserve to be State's football captain.

There was no one in the building when he got back to the infirmary. He looked glumly at the depressing, barren walls and the long row of empty beds. "Soapy was right when he tabbed it Terring's isolation ward," he murmured.

He sat down on a chair in the corner of the room and was leafing through a *Sports Illustrated* when one of the servers from the dining hall arrived with a tray of food. "I'll pick up the tray in the morning," the man said, setting it down on a nearby desk. "Enjoy."

Chip thanked him and leisurely ate the roast beef dinner. Now he was the only person in the building, and his only hope of companionship was a visit from Coach Ralston after skull practice. He walked over to the magazine rack and selected another magazine, opening it to the table of contents. He started at the top and read each one of the titles right through to the bottom of the page. "It's useless," he said, placing the magazine back in the metal rack. "I'm as bad as Hansen. All I can think about is football."

He selected a bed from the long line, adjusted the pillow, lay down, and closed his eyes. He let his thoughts wander for a time, but they always came back to Hansen. He and the tall fullback both had single-track minds when it came to football. But there was a difference. Hansen thought only about himself, while all Chip Hilton wanted was a good team and a winning season. Why couldn't Hansen think that way? The way Chip saw it, the position a fellow played on a team was unimportant. The big thing was to play where he could help the team most.

"Hansen is all wet anyway," he muttered aloud. "A lot of teams use variations of the *I* or the *T,* and the two backs who line up behind the quarterback are simply ball carriers, no matter whether Hansen calls one of them fullback or not. For the life of me, I don't get it. There has to be *some* kind of answer to this fullback mania."

His thoughts shifted to Speed Morris and Fireball Finley. Speed was listed as a halfback and Fireball as a fullback in the programs, but that was merely the traditional method of designating backfield positions. Speed was five-eleven in height and weighed 170 pounds while Fireball was an even six feet in height with a normal playing weight of 230 pounds. Just the same, both were running backs, ball carriers. The only difference between the two was sheer power. When that was needed, Fireball got the call.

Ball carriers had to have the fast start and be able to sprint through quick openings in the line, and have enough speed to turn the corners and break loose for the long runs. That wasn't all of it either. Running backs had to be durable, be able to change direction at full speed, and possess a change-of-pace ability deceptive enough to throw potential tacklers off balance. Hansen had *some* of these requisites, but Fireball and Speed had them all!

"This is stupid," he murmured. "I can't spend all my time in here thinking about Hansen. I've got to do something positive. I'll second-guess Coach and figure out his offensive and defensive teams. I don't think Doc will mind if I use the computer."

Chip swung his long legs to the floor and walked through the ward to the front office and sat down

behind Doc's iMac. He typed in the offensive-team positions and then added the names of the veterans in the
positions they had played the previous year. It was a
veteran offensive outfit with the starting lineup intact
from last year except for two positions, right guard and
right end.

OFFENSIVE TEAM

Tight End	Montague	6'3"	188 lbs.
Left Tackle	Cohen	6'4"	240 "
Left Guard	Anderson	5'8"	165 "
Center	Smith	6'0"	190 "
Right Guard	*Hansen*	*6'7"*	*200* "
Right Tackle	Maxim	6'2"	195 "
Split End	*Hazzard*	*6'3"*	*190* "
Quarterback	Hilton	6'4"	185 "
Flankerback	Jacobs	6'9"	190 "
Running Back	Morris	5'11"	170 "
Running Back	Finley	6'0"	220 "

Chip printed off the list and, using a pencil, wrote
in the names of Hansen and Hazzard in the vacant
spots. "Those two are a must," he declared. "Now for
the defensive unit. Or I guess I should say what's left
of it."

Chip swiveled his chair back in front of the computer and typed the positions. He entered the names of
Whittemore, O'Malley, and Roberts in the spots they
had played the previous year.

He studied the blank spaces on the screen and
shook his head skeptically. "No wonder Coach is worried," he muttered. He turned to the desk and wrote
down the names of the remaining players on a sepa-
rate sheet of paper. Then he compared each one of
these players with his offensive team counterpart. In
every case, with the exception of Whittemore, O'Malley,

and Roberts, the offensive team players were far superior in defensive abilities and experience.

Printing this second list and collecting the others, Chip walked back into the ward and sat down on the side of his bed. Then he placed names of the offensive team players in the vacant spots.

DEFENSIVE UNIT

Left End	Montague	6'3"	188 lbs.
Left Tackle	*Cohen*	*6'4"*	*240* "
Right Tackle	*Maxim*	*6'2"*	*195* "
Right End	Roberts	6'0"	190 "
Left Linebacker	O'Malley	5'10"	190 "
Middle Linebacker	*Hansen*	*6'7"*	*200* "
Right Linebacker	*Roberts (Riley)*	*6'0"*	*190* "
Left Cornerback	*Jacobs (Aker)*	*6'0"*	*190* "
Right Cornerback	*Finley*	*6'0"*	*220* "
Strong Safety	*Morris*	*5'11"*	*170* "
Free Safety	Hilton	*6'4"*	*185* "

Every player on the list was capable of playing both ways. In fact, it was nothing new for Biggie, Soapy, Speed, Finley, Maxim, and himself to play with the defensive unit. Even with the fine defensive team Coach Ralston had on hand the previous year, the six of them had been used in certain defensive situations.

Concentrating on the computer printouts, he checked the teams he had chosen once more. "There's no other way," he concluded aloud. "Most of us can expect to play both ways—or I don't know Coach Ralston."

A
One-Man Team

"WHAT DON'T you know about Ralston?"

Chip would have recognized that voice anywhere. He had been so deeply engrossed that he hadn't realized he was talking out loud again. When he looked up, Coach Curly Ralston and Doc Terring were walking down the long corridor toward him.

Chip got to his feet. "I've been trying to figure out what you're going to do about the defensive unit, Coach," he said.

"I wish I knew," Ralston said, shaking his head. "The Doc wants to take your temperature."

Terring tilted Chip's head and carefully inserted the thermometer in Chip's left ear. Coach Ralston sat down on the adjacent bed and waited quietly until Terring removed the thermometer. The physician glanced at the numbers and nodded. "Perfectly normal."

"Thank goodness," Ralston said. "Now, Chip, let's see that defensive team."

"I was just fooling around," Chip said, handing the papers to the coach.

While Ralston was studying the lineups, Chip appraised the likable coach. Ralston had keen eyes, a determined mouth, and a stubborn chin. He appeared to be gaunt, but this was belied by his wide shoulders and solid body. The head coach was a national authority on the game and a winner in all respects, but especially as a sportsman. Every player who had the opportunity to work under him appreciated his fairness and understanding. In addition to his personality and organizing ability, Ralston possessed the inner quality of mental toughness so vital to developing the winning habit.

"There's only one thing wrong, Chip," Ralston said thoughtfully. "And I'm quite sure you are aware of it. We can't afford to expose players like Morris and yourself to the game-after-game beating a defensive player takes. I *am* planning to use you and Morris as kickoff and punt receivers, but that's about it."

"Coach is right," Terring added. "Fellows like Cohen, Maxim, and Finley have the weight and stamina to take it. You and Morris just don't have the weight and strength."

"Now we come to Hansen," Ralston continued. "I know all about his ambition to play as a fullback, but he's just too valuable to use in a backup job. He's *got* to be a starter. But he's got a lot to learn as a middle linebacker. You can forget him as an offensive player. Right now, defense is our number-one problem."

"I can sure testify to Hansen's blitzing ability," Chip said dryly.

"You certainly can," Ralston said grimly. "His action today was inexcusable, but he can be a big help. If we can bring him around."

"I feel the same way, Coach."

"Think you can do anything with him?"

"I'm trying, sir."

"I know," Ralston said significantly. He handed Chip a sheaf of papers and continued. "We reviewed our variations of the *I* and *T* tonight and added some plays from the split-T. It might be a good idea for you to check them out. By the way, Doc and Murph Kelly both think you are trying to do too much. So do I."

"You were lucky last year," Terring said.

"I didn't miss any games."

"Just the same," Ralston said, "I agree with Doc. This year your luck might run out. No, Chip, we've got to limit your action. Have you ever stopped to check how many things you do for us?" Without waiting for a reply, he continued.

"First, you do all the kicking. Kickoffs, field goals, and points after touchdowns. You quarterback the offense and run and pass the ball. That should be enough for any two players. But you do even more. You often run back kickoffs and punts, and you've frequently played in the free-safety spot when our opponents have third down and long yardage. I ought to be kicked for letting you get away with it."

Ralston paused, and a quick smile of understanding swept across his lips. "I know exactly how you feel. And I know you are the most versatile football player I've ever coached, but *all* the coaches—Rockwell, Sullivan, Stewart, and Nelson—agree with Doc, Kelly, and myself. Your game action must be limited, or we stand a good chance of losing you altogether. And *that* we can't afford to do."

"Amen," Terring said.

"Now on Saturday," Ralston continued, "we're going to do a lot of experimenting. Classes start on Monday, and we play our first game the following Saturday, September 2. We've got to get a good, long look at some of our new candidates, and I don't plan to use you very much. I am sure you realize the importance of that decision."

"Of course, Coach. But I'm stronger than I was last year. I've spent a lot of time on weights and conditioning."

"Maybe, but you haven't put on a pound," Terring interrupted. "In fact, you've lost five pounds. You can't do it all, Chip. It takes eleven men to make a team."

"More like seventy-five," Ralston said.

"I know," Chip said. "But I played both ways in high school and with the frosh team and often last year with the varsity."

"We hope to change that this year," Ralston said. "Now, get some sleep, kiddo. See you tomorrow afternoon, I hope."

The two men left, and Chip remained sitting on his bed, thinking back through the conversation. Maybe he *was* trying to do too much, trying to be a one-man team. He had never really thought that way about it. He just wanted to play. Realizing he was still holding the papers Ralston had given him, he began to study the formations.

```
        O      O O X O O                    O
  X                X
                   X
                   X
```
I-Formation (Alignment No. 1)

```
        O      O O X O O                    O
  X                X
                 X     X
```
I-Formation (Alignment No. 2)

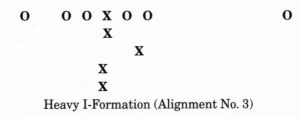

Heavy I-Formation (Alignment No. 3)

A number of the I-formation plays followed, but Chip spent little time with them. He wanted to check the split-T.

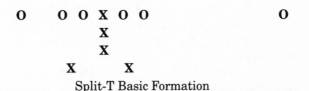

Split-T Basic Formation

"It's a great grind-it-out formation," Chip reflected, "but it also gives the quarterback a lot of protection and all kinds of options—handoffs to the running backs, the draw play, fake handoffs, keepers, lateral and forward passes, pitchouts, and end-around plays."

He studied all the plays State had used the previous year. Then he wrote in the names of the players he wanted to work with in the split-T.

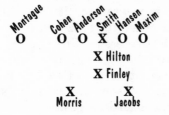

He started with Soapy at center. Soapy was really something as a center. He was perfect. The redhead always squared his shoulders and hips to the line of scrimmage, never lowered his body when he passed the ball back, and snapped the ball into the quarterback's hands fast, hard, and accurately. Soapy could block too. The two of them had practiced the pass from center hundreds of times, and they had never had a ball-exchange fumble in *any* game.

With Anderson and Hansen at the guards, Chip would have two fast and aggressive pullout linemen who could get out of the line and ahead of the ball carrier or fall back to protect the passing pocket. Hansen's height would provide a good screen on rollouts leading to keepers and passes, especially to the right, the side he liked to run.

Biggie and Maxim were naturals at the tackle positions. Both could slant charging guards or blitzing linebackers aside and away from a ball carrier or the passer. And on the short yardage plays, they could force almost any defensive player back a yard or two.

Montague was six-three and weighed 188 pounds. He excelled at the tight-end position because he was a fine blocker and a great pass receiver. Hazzard, the junior college graduate, also stood six-three. He somehow gave the impression of being fragile, but he weighed around 190 pounds, and his great speed and moves made him the best pass receiver in camp.

The backfield was a veteran outfit. Fireball and Speed couldn't be beat. When the blitz was on and the opponents' front four were pressing, Speed Morris was always in position for a safety pass in the flat.

"Yes," Chip breathed with satisfaction, "the split-T fits our offensive guys as if it were designed for us." He had placed Jacobs at flankerback position, but Aker was almost as good. Jacobs got the call because in addition to being a strong runner, he was an accurate left-handed passer.

He placed the papers on the table beside his bed, changed into his sweats, and tried to go to sleep. But he was restless, and it was long after he had turned out his lights that he fell asleep.

It seemed only a few minutes later when he was awakened by someone shaking his shoulder. "Chip! Wake up!" Soapy whispered hoarsely.

Chip sat up in bed and shook off the hand that grasped his shoulder. In the dim light of the ward, he made out the face of his best pal.

"Soapy!" he said. "What are you doing here? What time is it?"

"Nearly one o'clock, and you've got to hurry."

"Hurry? What for?"

"To stop Fireball and Hansen. They're going to fight it out."

"What? Fight? How did *you* find out about it?"

"Coach made us do ten laps after the meeting, and I was behind Fireball when Hansen passed me as if I was standing still."

"That was different," Chip deadpanned.

Soapy wrinkled his nose indignantly. "Say that again. Anyway, I took off after him and heard him ask Fireball if he was as tough off the field as he tried to be on it."

"What was he talking about?"

"Fighting! Anyway, Fireball tried to laugh him off, but then Hansen called him yellow."

"What happened then?"

"You know Fireball. He blew his stack and called Hansen a poor sport and said he would meet him any-place and anytime."

"That doesn't sound like Fireball, Soapy. Hansen hasn't got a chance with him. Fireball is the conference wrestling champion and a good boxer besides. I can't believe he would try to hurt Hansen."

"Maybe not. Anyway, Hansen said for Fireball to meet him at the boat house at one o'clock and to come alone."

"What time is it now? How much time do we have?"

"About five minutes if you hurry."

"How do you know Fireball will meet him?" Chip asked, tying his running shoes.

"Because I went to bed with my clothes on and pretended to be asleep. Then, when Fireball sneaked out of his bunk, I hurried over here."

"Anyone see you?"

"No! Come on, Chip."

"All right, I'm ready. Let's go."

Soapy led the way out of the infirmary and past the dining hall and soon they were beyond the realm of the dim light that illuminated the camp buildings. A bank of storm clouds hid the moon and the sky was pitch black. Soapy slowed the pace, and Chip's thoughts raced ahead to the boat house. He was thinking it was too dark to see a guy clearly, much less hit him. "It'll probably just end up in a wrestling match," he concluded under his breath. "How much farther?" he asked.

Soapy lifted Chip's arm and pointed to the right. "Just ahead," he whispered. "See it?"

Chip focused his eyes in the direction Soapy indicated. In a second the boat house, an even darker presence against the darkness, became visible. It was about fifty feet ahead.

CHAPTER 4

The Heisman Trophy

CHIP TOOK the lead until he could see the boat house and two shadowy figures. He stopped Soapy with his arm. "Go on back to the cabin," he whispered. "I can take care of this better if I'm alone."

"No way!" Soapy whispered fiercely. "I'll wait right here by this tree until I'm sure everything is all right."

"OK, but don't make any noise."

Chip moved forward a few feet until he could distinguish one figure from the other. Fireball and Hansen were shedding their shirts and talking at the same time. Chip paused to listen.

"This is plain stupid," Fireball growled.

"Not to me!" Hansen retorted. "You made me look bad this afternoon. Now it's my turn."

"What did you expect? That was football. But this! Why, this is sheer nonsense. Kid stuff! You want a fight, so I'll give you a go. But I still don't know what we're fighting about. The only reason I'm here is because you called me yellow. I won't take that from anyone. Now, what kind of fight do you want? A stand-up fight or what?"

Hansen did not answer, and so Fireball continued. "You're going to get the same thing you got this afternoon, only worse."

"Maybe," Hansen said grimly. "Anyway, anything goes."

"You asked for it," Fireball said. "Let's go."

Chip didn't wait any longer. The two players were moving closer together as he dashed forward. "Hold it!" he demanded.

But he was too late. Hansen made a wild swing that Fireball parried easily. Then, charging forward, Fireball ducked under Hansen's arms. Hitting his tall opponent around the knees, Fireball dumped Hansen on the ground with a wrestler's perfect takedown. Hansen twisted and turned, but Fireball ended up on top and pinned the furious opponent's shoulders to the ground.

Chip arrived at that moment and grabbed Fireball around the arm. Pulling him back up, he lifted the burly fullback to his feet.

"It's OK, Chip," Fireball said. "I wasn't going to hurt—"

It was as far as Fireball got. Hansen scrambled to his feet and smashed a hard right to Fireball's face. Then a flying body cut Hansen's feet out from under him for the second time in less than a minute.

"I've got him, Chip," Soapy yelled.

"Let him up," Chip said, "but keep him away for a second."

Chip pushed Fireball farther back. "I didn't expect you would have any part of a thing like this, Fireball," he said.

"What could I do? He called me yellow."

"Everyone knows you're not yellow. You didn't have to do anything!"

Soapy was standing in front of Hansen. Chip walked around him and grasped Hansen by the arm. "What's wrong with you, Hansen? You know how Coach feels about fighting."

"Take your hand off my arm," Hansen said ominously.

"Sure," Chip said. "Of course. But I can't stand by and see you two get bounced off the squad. If you had had a real fight tonight after what Coach said this afternoon, he would *have* to drop you. You can't possibly want that! Right or wrong?"

"Right, I guess," Hansen said.

"I think you and Fireball ought to shake hands and forget it." Chip turned to face Fireball. "Are you willing to shake hands?"

Fireball hesitated only a second. Then, stepping forward, he extended his hand. "Sure," he said. "Why not?"

Hansen backed away. "No," he said. "Not a chance. You started it right after I ran into Hilton. I didn't even see you coming."

"I didn't see you coming either," Chip said pointedly.

"Makes no difference," Hansen said. "I apologized to you for that, but Finley started slugging me before I could even turn around. He owes me an apology."

Finley turned abruptly away. "All right," he said over his shoulder, "if that's all you want, you've got it. I apologize."

"Hold up, Fireball," Chip said. "Soapy's going with you. Now listen. This whole thing ends here. No talking to anyone. Right?"

"Of course," Fireball said. "There's nothing to talk about. Nothing to fight about either."

Soapy joined Fireball, and side by side they walked away and into the darkness, leaving Chip and Hansen.

"Now what?" Hansen asked.

"I think you and I should do some talking," Chip replied quietly.

"What about?"

"About you and Fireball, for one thing."

"That's personal. How come you're out here? I thought you were in the infirmary."

"I am. But I had to come out here to stop you and Finley from making fools of yourselves."

"How did you find out about it? Did Finley tell you?"

"Fireball didn't tell me anything."

"What about Smith? How come you and he happened to show up? What were you going to do, gang up on me?"

"That would hardly be necessary," Chip remarked dryly. "No, Soapy heard you talking to Fireball while you were running around the track. He woke me up and told me about it in the infirmary just a few minutes ago. Fireball didn't even know Soapy heard you."

"You and your gang," Hansen said contemptuously. "I never saw so many cliques in my life."

"You seem to have one of your own," Chip said thoughtfully.

"Of course. What would you expect?"

"*We're* not a clique. Soapy and Biggie and Speed and I have been friends ever since we were kids back in Valley Falls. Fireball has been a close friend ever since I came to State."

"How about the way everyone gangs up in the chow line and in the dining room?"

"Gangs up? What do you mean?"

"It's like everybody has their own little groups. You know, the way you line up to get food and where everybody sits. Anybody who's new is left out, and left to last."

"That's been going on for years. It's a tradition."

"It's a pretty lousy one."

"I agree. However, I never thought much about it along those lines."

"You're the captain. Why don't you do something about it?"

"I will. Now what's with you and Finley?"

"I told you before. It's none of your business."

"That's where you're wrong. It's very much my business. Part of a captain's job is to create harmony and develop team spirit. Besides, Hansen, the team needs you."

"Needs *me?*"

"That's right. You're the only player in camp who can play middle linebacker the way it ought to be played. Coach Ralston said that tonight when he visited me in the infirmary. Mike Ryan played that position for Coach last year. You're so much better than he was. There's no comparison.

"Coach Ralston has built a national reputation as a defensive genius, and he's been offered a half dozen professional jobs for that very reason. He's counting on you to lead his defensive team."

"But I'm a fullback."

"He knows that. But surely you can't expect him to demote Fireball. Why, he's been playing in that position for three years. One year on the frosh team and two on the varsity. And he's good."

"What about Morris, then? What makes Ralston think he's a better running back than I am?"

"Speed is a different kind of back. He's lightning fast. He breaks away at least once in just about every game and he goes all the way. He's great on pitchouts and once he's past the line of scrimmage, he simply outruns the opponents' secondary. Remember, too, he and Fireball and I have worked together for two years. Another thing: Speed is great on screen passes. He can read the field, and he's always in the right place to receive the ball. Finally, he picks up his blockers and runs to daylight almost every time."

"What about the reverse fullback position, then?" Hansen persisted.

"Coach mentioned that tonight. He said you were too valuable to the team to be a backup player. He said you had to be a starter. Personally, I think you could play both ways. Middle linebacker and pullout guard."

"You and Finley and Morris," Hansen said bitterly. "They make you a great quarterback, and you want me for a pullout guard to make you an even greater one. Well, let me tell *you* something. I won't play offensive guard for anyone. For Ralston or you or anyone else.

"Another thing. You and Finley aren't the only quarterback–fullback combination in the world. Whip Ward and I were good enough to play on a junior college team that was undefeated for two years and national champions besides. State has never done that! And as far as honors are concerned, both of us were JuCo all-Americans. For two years!"

"Coach Ralston knows that, Hansen. So do I. But there is a big difference between junior college all-Americans and university all-Americans. In my opinion, you can make all-American as a middle linebacker on the college level, which is right where you can help the team most and where Coach needs help most."

"Maybe so, but a guy has a right to play where he likes to play, doesn't he? I like soccer just about as much as football and if it wasn't for—" Hansen stopped in the middle of his sentence and walked over to the boat house, slumping down on the bench beside the door.

Chip followed him and quietly sat down beside him. He sensed that Hansen had been on the verge of saying something that would reveal the reason for his unusual behavior. "If it wasn't for what?" Chip asked gently.

Hansen shook his head. "Never mind," he said. "Anyway, when Nik Nelson talked to Whip and Hazzard and Riley and me about coming to State, he said we were sure to play our regular positions. So far, I haven't had a fair chance and neither has Whip. I want some action. I love football, and I want to play."

"When Coach Nelson talked to you, he had no idea that you would turn out to be a great linebacker. You said something about wanting action. Well, middle linebackers get more action than any player on the field. Besides, if you wanted to, you could play both ways. How many college players can you name who do that?"

"You do it! So do Finley and Cohen."

"Not all the time like you will. You don't know Coach Ralston very well, but I do. And I know that the greatest compliment he can give any player is to place him in charge of State's defense. The middle linebacker backs up all the running plays through the line, intercepts passes, blocks kicks, dumps quarterbacks, and calls the defensive strategy. Where can you get more action than that?"

Hansen had listened to Chip without a word. When Chip finished, he nodded his head. "Maybe so," he said stubbornly, "but I just happen to believe in myself as much as you believe in yourself. And I believe I am just as good at the fullback position as any college player in the country. By the way, have you ever heard of the Heisman Trophy?"

For a split second, Chip thought Hansen was putting him on. He sure had heard of it. Hadn't everyone heard of it? In fact, Chip had won that honor as a sophomore. Recovering quickly, he nodded. "Yes," he responded evenly, "I have."

"Well then, answer me three questions: Who selects the guy who gets it? How long have they been giving it? And how many linemen have ever won it?"

"I know the award is given out by the Downtown Athletic Club in New York City and that sportswriters all over the country select the winner," Chip said. "I know that much, but I have no idea how long they have been doing it or how many linemen have won it."

"Well, *I* do. I was reading about it just the other day. Just two linemen have ever won it, one in 1936 and the other in 1949. The sportswriters have been giving the award since 1935, and in all that time, only two, now, get it, *only two linemen,* have ever won it. All the rest were backs or wide receivers. And you're trying to tell me that linemen are important. Hogwash! I want to play pro ball after graduation, and fullbacks are as important as quarterbacks in the pro draft."

"It takes eleven players in eleven different positions to make a team in the pros as well as in college," Chip countered.

"I know that. But I also know that the least Ralston could do is give me a chance to show what I can do as a back."

"I think he will in time. But right now, I think you ought to play ball with him and help out where he needs help."

"I don't owe Ralston a thing," Hansen said quietly. "Nor State," he added. "And I don't have to play football." He deliberated for a second and then continued. "I can quit football. And if I don't get a chance to play fullback at least part of the game at Eastern, I might do just that."

"Why the Eastern State game?" Chip asked.

"Because my parents grew up in Eastern," Hansen said impulsively.

"What's the difference where you play? The middle linebacker is the most important position in football."

"Maybe. Anyway, it's a personal matter."

"Look, Hansen. I'm not trying to pry into your personal affairs. I'm just thinking about the team. Let's forget personalities and positions and see what happens on Saturday. All right?"

Hansen nodded and the players started back toward the cabins. When they reached the edge of the dimly lighted camp area, Chip said good night, but Hansen did not reply. The tall newcomer turned away and trudged toward his bunk and disappeared into the darkness.

Chip walked across the gravel path to the infirmary. He had made no progress with the surly fullback, and he felt foolish and discouraged. *He is ruining everything,* Chip vented silently. Hansen wasn't interested in loyalty to the team or the coach or even to State. Why continue a losing battle? Nothing was going to change Greg Hansen. Why try? Forget Hansen!

Yet Chip knew his venting had to stop there. He wasn't allowed to end a problem that way, even if it was tempting. "I don't know the whole story," he reminded himself. "I need to give Hansen the benefit of the doubt, whether I want to or not. He deserves that, and it wouldn't be fair if I wrote him off. Period."

With a sigh, Chip reflected on how easy it was to become engulfed in a mind-set of beating Greg, of showing him up. *But I can do better, and with God's help I will,* he told himself firmly.

With that he prayed for patience in the days ahead and then continued on to his cabin.

CHAPTER 5

Building Team Spirit

DOC TERRING released Chip from the infirmary Thursday afternoon with instructions for him to report to Murph Kelly for a light workout. Kelly assigned him to thirty minutes of weights, a long run around the track, and a few quick starts. Later the trainer let him pass the ball and take a turn at punting. After a half-hour of punting, Kelly told him to report back to Terring for a final checkup.

Terring's checkup was brief but thorough. "All right, Chip," he said at last. "Get your things and beat it."

"I'm gone, Doc," Chip said, sighing in relief. "Thanks for everything."

"Take it easy tomorrow."

"Right!" Chip said, flashing the doctor a quick grin. Gathering up his things, he headed for the cabin he shared with Speed, Soapy, Biggie, Fireball, Anderson, Montague, and Whittemore. It was good to be back in their cabin. He dropped down on his bed to wait for the guys. An hour later, his pals ran up the wooden steps

and barged into the cabin. They immediately surrounded his bed.

"Country club living!" Soapy said, roughing up
Chip's mop of blond hair. "Tea and toast and afternoon
naps. I think I'll get *me* a concussion!"

"You've had one for years," Speed jested, pushing
the redhead out of the way. "You all right, Chip?"

"Of course, I'm all right."

"It was my fault," Speed said ruefully. "I saw
Hansen coming, but I had to hang onto the ball. I
couldn't do a thing."

"I know," Chip said understandingly. "It's a wonder
you didn't get bowled over too."

Biggie was studying Chip closely. "Hansen clob-
bered you good," he said seriously.

"Yeah, he jarred me up a bit," Chip admitted.

"Running into a kicker is stupid," Biggie growled.

"Ralston didn't like it," Speed said. "Hansen doesn't
know how close he was to getting the gate."

"*That* will be taken care of on Saturday," Monty said
pointedly.

"Nothing doing!" Chip said quickly. "It's all over."

"Fireball handled him as if he were a blocking
dummy on that kickoff play," Speed said. "Did you see
Hansen land on his backside?"

"I said it was all over," Chip repeated firmly. "Come
on, let's get on the chow line."

The players were lining up as they approached the
dining room, and Hansen's reference to the ganging-up
came back to Chip. The chow line had formed in the
same order for so many years that it had become a tradition. The offensive and defensive starters gathered
at the head of the line with the reserve letterman
closely behind them. The junior college grads and the
previous year's scrubs followed. Last, but far from
least, Chip was thinking, were the sophomores.

The line was formed in the same order now, and as Chip walked toward the front porch of the dining room, the friendly greetings were so sincere that his chest tightened with emotion.

Skip Miller's nod and smile were the friendliest of all. Miller had starred at quarterback for the previous year's freshman team. A resident of University, where State was located, Miller had adopted Chip's quarterback style while still playing in high school. He had worked so hard at perfecting it that their moves, ballhandling, and passing were almost identical. Many of the State fans had difficulty telling them apart, and some people even mistook them for brothers. Both were now six-four in height and weighed in the neighborhood of 185 pounds, and each had blond hair. The chief difference was the color of their eyes. Chip's eyes were gray whereas Skip's were sky blue.

Camp food was served cafeteria style, and the chow-line formation carried into the dining room. As Chip walked along the serving counter and toward the table where his buddies usually sat, he realized, for the first time, the impression the chow line and the table groupings must make on newcomers. Hansen was right! He placed his tray on the table and looked around the room. "It's all wrong," he said.

"What's all wrong?" Soapy asked.

"This!" Chip said, gesturing toward the various tables. "We say we're trying to develop team spirit, yet we defeat it with the very first camp meal. Instead of lining up according to seniority and eating separately, we should mix with the new guys—the sophomores and the junior college grads."

"Sure!" Soapy agreed. "Let's make friends! We should spread out and sit with different guys. That way we can help develop team spirit. I know, we'll call it the 'Soapy Smith Camp Sundown Socializing Project!' How's that?"

"The name's a bit much, but the idea is good," Speed offered, patting Soapy on the back. Speed cocked his head in the direction of the line and grinned at Fireball. "Finley, you go sit beside Hansen."

"Not me!" Fireball retorted. "*You* sit beside him."

The after-dinner schedule never varied. Murph Kelly always led the squad on a brisk walk and always dismissed the athletes with the same words: "It is now 7:15. Skull practice begins at eight o'clock sharp. Be there at 7:55 or be ready for laps right after the meeting."

Kelly seldom found it necessary to impose the penalty. Ralston was a stickler for promptness, and the players respected him and his mandates. Chip and the guys from his cabin arrived for skull practice ten minutes early with their notebooks under their arms. They waited outside the recreation hall until the rest of the squad arrived and then began to put Soapy's socializing project into practice. Separating, they took seats beside or near the new guys. Chip found a chair beside Hazzard.

Curly Ralston and the rest of his staff arrived right on time. Nelson and Stewart pulled one of the portable whiteboards to the center of the stage. Ralston lifted a hand for silence and the players quieted. "I realize you are thinking ahead to the breakup game," he said, "so we will start with the lineups. The teams you see listed on the board will work together tomorrow morning and afternoon. Coaches Rockwell and Sullivan will be in charge of team A, and Coaches Stewart and Nelson will work with team B.

"Now, write the names of the players and the positions in your notebooks."

OFFENSIVE POSITIONS	TEAM A	TEAM B
Tight End	Montague	Williams
Left Tackle	Cohen	Gilman
Left Guard	Anderson	Turner
Center	Smith	Riley
Right Guard	O'Malley	Spencer
Right Tackle	Maxim	Roth
Split End	Whittemore	Hazzard
Quarterback	Hilton	Ward
Flankerback	Jacobs	Kerr
Running Back	Morris	Miller
Running Back	Finley	Hansen

Copying the names into his notebook, Chip studied team A's offensive lineup. It was practically a veteran team. The only weak spots were at right guard and at right end. O'Malley was strong and tough, but he wasn't fast enough to pull out of the line and lead the ball carriers on outside plays.

Whittemore was a good defensive end but lacked the speed required of an offensive split end. Glancing at team B's offensive lineup, he noted with some satisfaction that Ward and Hansen would, at last, get a chance to work as a quarterback–fullback combination.

DEFENSIVE POSITIONS	TEAM A	TEAM B
Left End	Whittemore	Williams
Left Tackle	Cohen	Gilman
Right Tackle	Maxim	King
Right End	Johnson	Spencer
Left Linebacker	Aker	Turner
Middle Linebacker	McCarthy	Hansen
Right Linebacker	Roberts	Roth
Left Cornerback	O'Malley	Kerr
Right Cornerback	Finley	Gerow
Strong Safety	Morris	Ward
Free Safety	Hilton	Miller

He checked the defensive assignments. McCarthy was a good backup tackle and a good possibility for the middle linebacker job. *But he isn't in Hansen's class when it comes to speed and savvy,* Chip reflected. With the exception of Finley, Hansen was the only player in camp who could really fill that position. It was a cinch, however, that Ralston wasn't going to expose Fireball to a beating *both* ways.

When the players had entered the teams in their notebooks, Coach Ralston turned the shiny whiteboard around and began his lecture. Starting with the I-formation, he explained the strengths and weaknesses of each of its alignments and diagrammed several plays that were particularly effective. He followed the I-formation with the basic-T and, last but far from least, in Chip's opinion anyway, the split-T.

It was a long session. Coach Ralston believed that repetition was the secret of perfection, and he translated that belief into action. He stressed over and over again the importance of timing and the fakes and moves every offensive player must make if the play was to go. It was after nine o'clock when he finished. Then he gave the squad a fifteen-minute break.

When time was up, the coaches pulled another whiteboard to the middle of the platform. The material listed was the same that the players had entered in their notebooks during the first week of camp. Chip studied it while Ralston waited for the players to get settled.

OFFENSIVE BIBLE

RUNNING GAME
>   Inside plays (traps)
>   Outside plays (sweeps and reverses)
>>   Pullout guards in interference
>   Goal-line plays against stacked offenses
>   Delayed plays
>>   Backfield reverses
>>   End around
>>   Splits
>>   Keepers
>>   Draw plays
>>   Statue of Liberty
>   The extra point
>>   Placekick
>>   2-pointers (runs and passes)

PASSING GAME
>   Pass Patterns
>>   Passes in the flat
>>   Sideline passes
>>   Over the middle
>>   Safety-valve passes
>>   Buttonhooks
>>   Screen passes
>>   Long passes (the bomb and the fly)
>>   Extra-point passes (the 2-pointers)

KICKING GAME (with and against the wind)
>   Kickoffs
>>   High kicks and low kicks
>>   Short onside kicks
>>   Medium onside kicks
>>   Punts
>   Point after touchdown
>   Receiving kickoffs (formations)
>>   Funnel (wedge)
>>   Upfield blocking
>>   Halfbacks in restraining zone
>>   Runback plays

The players quieted, and Ralston gestured toward the board. "You have this outline in your notebooks," he said, "and Coach Rockwell will review it tonight. Coach Sullivan will review the defense tomorrow night. Before you leave camp, you must have your notebook completed. You will turn it in to Coach Rockwell Sunday morning. It will be returned to you Monday afternoon after practice at University Stadium. All right, Rock, take over."

Coach Rockwell stood five-ten in height, weighed about 175 pounds, and was lean and muscular. *He doesn't look a day older,* Chip reflected. *Same black hair and eyes, same quick steps, same vibrant voice, and the same passion for coaching.*

Watching Rockwell move to the whiteboard, Chip's thoughts raced back to his hometown and his high-school days. Rockwell had retired from Valley Falls High School the year Chip and his friends graduated. Coach Ralston and State's athletic director, Dad Young, had immediately snapped Rockwell up as an assistant in athletics.

The veteran coach had mentored Chip and his pals through four years of football, basketball, and baseball at Valley Falls High School and then continued to work with them here at State. Chip knew that Rockwell had given them something far more precious than the myriad athletic skills he had helped them develop. He had molded vital character qualities in them during their formative years. He had instilled in them honesty, accountability, sportsmanship, leadership, and compassion. Together with the Lord and his mom, Mary Hilton, Henry Rockwell had guided Chip well.

Although Rockwell was listed as State's offensive coach, every player on the squad knew that Ralston considered the veteran his chief assistant. Beginning with the inside plays and the slanting, traps, and blocking each required, Rockwell explained the part that each phase played in Ralston's overall offensive philosophy.

The players had spent hours studying their notebooks; they had practiced the plays on the field, first in slow motion, next at half speed, and finally at game speed. Now they were learning the whys and wherefores behind the moves they were perfecting. Finishing with the running plays, Rockwell went into all phases of State's intricate passing game. Then he discussed the importance of kicking, stressing that kicking was considered a part of the offense.

When he finished the kicking review, Rockwell glanced toward Ralston. The head coach looked at his watch and nodded. "Take five more minutes, Rock."

Rockwell then commented on the duties and responsibilities of the running backs and the coordination and timing required between the offensive linemen and the backs. "With the exception of our wide end," he said, "we play our line against the opponent's front four. Since we have a six-man line opposing their four front men, we should be able to contain them. The width of the spaces between our offensive linemen varies, of course.

"We try to spread the opponent's defensive linemen as much as possible. However, when the opponent's defensive front four will not spread, our linemen must set up closer together. Now let's assume that our linemen have done their jobs and have been able to handle their opponents on our running plays. That brings us to the ball carriers.

"Ball carriers must be sure blockers, possess good hands, and be able to hold onto the ball whether it's from a handoff, a pitchout, or a pass. The line does the heavy work, but *every* back has a definite move, fake, or blocking assignment on *every* play."

The coach's eyes roamed the room, making contact with player after player as Rockwell continued. "Running backs must assume the responsibility of protecting the passer. If a linebacker does not come through on the rush or blitz, the ball carrier on that side goes out into the flat for a safety pass. With the defensive big four out of the way, a fleet back can often break into the opponent's secondary through sheer speed and quickness.

"The power back usually breaks loose because of his strength and drive. He is usually bigger and often faster than most secondary defenders, and once he is past the defensive team's big four, he can pick up extra yardage on second and even third efforts to advance." He paused and gestured toward a player sitting in the second row. Smiling, he continued. "Speedsters like Morris get loose because they are the fastest and quickest runners we have."

Rockwell paused again and turned to Ralston. "That's about it, Chief."

"Thanks, Rock," Ralston said. "Good job. Now, it's 10:30, and you men have been very patient. So the coaching staff has decided to reward you with a late sleep-in tomorrow morning. Breakfast will be served at 9:30 and practice at 11:00. Light gear. That's it! Good night."

The players had been sitting quietly for a long time. Now they could no longer contain their exuberance. Yelling and pushing, playfully elbowing one another aside, they broke for the door, relieved and happy that the tiresome listening and fighting to stay alert were finished. All were thankful that there would be only one more session before the breakup game and the end of camp.

Chip and Hazzard were the last players to leave the recreational hall. They were discussing State's passing patterns. When they came out of the building, Chip saw that Soapy and Speed were walking along with some of the sophomores. Biggie, Monty, Whitty, Anderson, and Fireball were kidding around with Riley. And, far ahead of everyone, hurrying toward their cabin, were Hansen and Ward. Chip figured he knew what that meant. They were in a hurry to make plans for Saturday afternoon.

CHAPTER 6

Number-One Enemy

THE SLEEP-IN privilege was a welcome break from the rigorous training camp routine, but only a few of the players took advantage of the opportunity. Many swam in the lake or hiked along the mountain paths. A few simply lolled around until it was time for breakfast. Chip, Speed, Biggie, and Soapy separated and mixed in with the different groups. Chip sensed a feeling of squad warmth for the first time.

"It's a good beginning," he mused, "but we need to keep it going."

The morning workout was light, consisting of football calisthenics, wind sprints, and group work in kicking, passing, and running signals. In the afternoon, the coaches of the A and B teams devoted the practice chiefly to plays and defensive alignments. Dinner that night was especially noisy, but under all the talk and laughter, a feeling of tension was beginning to build up. The breakup game meant the moment of truth for many of the players.

With the first regular game of the season only a week away, the breakup game would be the deciding factor in determining which players would be cut from the squad and which players would be issued varsity uniforms on Monday.

When the players assembled that night in the recreation hall, Coach Sullivan was ready for them. He waited until the players were settled and then nodded toward the whiteboard. "The first diagram outlines our basic defensive formation," he explained. "The second is the ten-man rush we use when our opponents must kick or we need the ball and are willing to gamble to get it. It is a dangerous defense because, as you can see, our secondary moves up right behind the line and we have only one man back."

Basic Defense

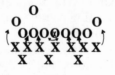

Ten-Man Rush Defense

Sullivan gave the players time to copy the formations in their notebooks before resuming the session. "The basic defense is composed of three lines. The front line consists of two ends and two tackles, and they are generally known as the front four. The ends are numbered 1 and 4 and the tackles are numbered 2 and 3.

"Cohen, suppose you tell us the responsibilities of the front four."

From across the room, Soapy's glance at Chip expressed his amusement. Biggie Cohen, the gentle giant, was a person of few words. He preferred action to words when it came to football or anything else important to him. He rose to his feet and said, "Well, Coach, we're supposed to stop the other team's line attack and rush the passers and kickers. We're also expected to chase runners and passers no matter where they go."

Biggie sat down and Sullivan continued. "Our second line includes the left linebacker, number 6; the right linebacker, number 7; and the middle linebacker, number 5. Finley often doubles as fullback on the offense and as a cornerback on the defense, but he has also played in a linebacker position. Suppose you discuss a linebacker's responsibility, Finley."

Fireball loved to back up a line. He ate up hard contact and bruising play. He rose from his folding chair and spoke clearly and authoritatively. "Linebackers are supposed to support the front four in stopping the opponent's line attacks. They also help in rushing passers and kickers. Their main job is to stop the other team's ground game. Next to the middle linebacker, the outside linebacker positions are the toughest of all to do well.

"The outside linebacker must defend and hold his position in most cases, but if there is no action in the line, he must help out wherever he is needed."

Fireball sat down, and Sullivan deliberated a second before speaking. "Now," he said, "we come to the middle linebacker. This player is expected to do just about everything there is do to on defense. He faces the brunt of all the opponent's power plunges through the line, most of the time with a big blocker leading the ball carrier. He's the leader of the blitz. He has to be big enough and fast enough to rush passers and quick enough to defend the middle passing zone behind the line. That is the toughest passing area of all to defend because the opposing team's ends and flankers can get there so quickly.

"The middle linebacker is the key to the team's entire defense. He has the toughest job in football and, defensively, the most important. No team will get far without a first-class middle linebacker.

"The middle linebacker keys on the opposing fullback for draw plays and inside line plunges. He is in on 80 percent of the tackles in most games and makes 25 to 30 percent of them personally. He quarterbacks the defensive alignment, leads the rush, intercepts passes, forces fumbles, and often nails the quarterback or ball carrier in his tracks.

"He must calculate the down, the yard line, the time left to play, the score, the offensive alignment, and the wind, and he must anticipate the play the opposing quarterback likes to use in a given situation. He is the number-one enemy of the offense and, as he goes, so goes his team's defense.

"The blitz is his big job. Height is important here because a tall middle linebacker can look down on the opposing team's backfield and figure the play. The middle linebacker is the man the offensive quarterback has to beat, and the two of them wage a personal duel from the opening to the closing plays of the game.

"Now I think your captain should say a few words about this enemy who faces him every time he lines up behind the center. As I said before, he is the man the quarterback must outwit all through the game. Take over, Hilton."

Chip knew that Coach Sullivan was talking indirectly to Hansen, and he wanted to help out. He had told Hansen just about the same thing the night they had talked at the lake, but the duel idea was a little different approach.

"Coach Sullivan is right about the duel," he said. "When I'm in the huddle and call a running play or a pass, it's always the middle linebacker I worry about. He's the one who causes our offense the most trouble. Almost every time I come out of the huddle and take my position behind Soapy, I find him staring me straight in the eyes as if he's trying to read my mind.

"Some of them must possess mental telepathy because they read the plays so accurately. Lots of times they shift to the very spot where the play is supposed to go.

"When that happens, it upsets everyone because I have to use audible signals and call a new play. The audible has to be given in a hurry, too, or we get penalized for taking too much time. Next to reading the other team's defense, the biggest problem I have is figuring when the middle linebacker is going to blitz.

"On third down with long yardage needed, I know it's a blitz situation. Then, if I think I've got it figured right, I call a draw play or a screen pass. But I have to be sure. Any way you look at it, the middle linebacker is the offensive quarterback's biggest headache.

"I try to figure out how good he is on the very first play we try from scrimmage. That's where Fireball or Speed help out. If I send them through the line, they come back to the huddle and tell me how he reacted.

Then I try him again. After two or three plays, I know about how tough he is and just about how much trouble he is going to give us."

Chip paused. "I guess that's it, Coach."

"Thanks, Hilton," Sullivan said. "Now let's get into our secondary. Our third line of defense is concerned with the left and right cornerbacks and our strong-safety player. The cornerbacks line up head to head or one on one against the opponent's split end and flankerback and stick with them no matter where they go. It's a tough assignment. Occasionally, but not often, we use the switch. The switch occurs when wide receivers cross over to the opposite side of the field.

"That brings us to the strong-safety man. I don't know a better one than Speed Morris. Speed, suppose you tell us about the strong-safety player's job."

By now, this was old stuff to Speed. It wasn't the first time Sullivan had put him on the spot. Speed was a pre-law student who had learned to handle speaking situations well. He waded right into it. "My job is to take care of the middle running and passing areas," he said wryly. "It's a tough job. Most opposing quarterbacks send a pass receiver into this area on every play, either as a decoy or as an actual receiver, and I have to be careful not to commit myself too quickly. Of course, if we have a good middle linebacker like Ace Gibbons, my job is much easier. Ace was the middle linebacker my sophomore year, and he was great! Mike Ryan played there last year and he was, well, just a little too eager." Speed shrugged his shoulders. "That's all, I guess."

Speed sat down and Sullivan took over again. "Now we come to the free safety. He is responsible for the deep areas and shifts to any position he thinks will be most helpful. It's a difficult job because he's expected to stop the long run and the long pass, the fly or the bomb. He must be able to anticipate plays and passes, possess sure tackling ability, and demonstrate all-around defensive instinct. Hilton alternated in that position last year and will undoubtedly share the responsibility again this year. You're on, Chip."

"I like to play the free-safety position," Chip explained. "A fellow is on his own in this position and matches wits with the quarterback just as the middle linebacker does. He has to watch the breakaway runners and key on the speedy long-pass receivers who can win a game almost anytime they can latch onto the ball.

"I think the free safety is the best defensive position of all. He's in charge of the last-chance defense and, consequently, should make more pass interceptions than any other player. He has to be familiar with the plays the opposing quarterbacks use on all downs and particularly those they like to use on third downs. Our coaches up in the booth help me out because they know the quarterback better than I do, and they can see the formations better. As you know, they phone information down to the bench, and it's relayed to the middle linebacker and free-safety player through hand signals, the same signals we've been working through this past week.

"When the other team has a wide end or a flanker-back who can run the hundred in ten seconds or less, it means the cornerback must have help. The free safety usually doubles up on this kind of a receiver. We know all these players from our scouting notes, but they have the advantage because they know the pattern that will be used and where the ball will be thrown. When we are up against two of these fast receivers, we use the blitz or a strong-side zone or some kind of a combination defense. There's a lot more, but it gives you an idea of the problems he faces."

"That's fine, Hilton," Sullivan said. "I'll finish it up." He turned the board around. "I know exactly how difficult it is for you to sit and listen to all this talking and explaining, but it has to be done." He pointed to the outline on the board. "Check the outline on the board with the one you have in your notebooks."

DEFENSIVE BIBLE

KICKOFFS
    Positions of players
    Responsibilities
    Safety Measures
    Long Kicks
    Short onside kicks
    Medium onside kicks
PUNTS
    Blitzing (see below)

    Blocking tacklers
    Protection
    Runback plays
GOAL-LINE STANDS
    Formations
STOPPING RUNNING OFFENSES
    Formations
    Personnel duties
    Stunting (Linebackers)
PASS DEFENSE
    Formations
    Player Responsibilities
    Double-teaming
    Zone alignment
    Combinations
BLITZING
    Passers
    Kickers (punts)
    Placekicks

SHOTGUN DEFENSE
    Formations
    Halfbacks
SHORT GAINS DEFENSE
LONG GAINS DEFENSE
DEFENDING SPLIT-T
DEFENSING THE I
DEFENSING STRAIGHT T
DEFENSING
    DOUBLE-WING
DEFENSING THE FLY
DEFENSING THE BOMB

Coach Sullivan gave the players time to check their notebooks and then asked if there were any questions. There were none. "I suggest you hit the sack. Tomorrow is a big day, and you will want to be well rested. We eat at eleven o'clock and dress at one. Be on time."

CHAPTER 7

Camp
Breakup Game

PLAYER BENCHES at Camp Sundown were located at the fifty-yard line on each side of the field. A set of low, wooden benches stood on the south side of the field, and these were crammed with spectators. Behind the rope fence on the north side of the field, cars were parked side by side from goal line to goal line.

Although it was only an intrasquad game, there were a number of sportswriters and university administrators ready for some State football action. Chip located Mr. Grayson, his employer, almost as soon as he reached the field. Mr. Grayson was sitting beside Mrs. Grayson and Mitzi Savrill. In addition to being an understanding employer, George Grayson was a State University alumni. He was a tremendous sports enthusiast, and he was proud of the State University athletes who worked in his store—including Soapy, Fireball, Whitty, and Chip, among others.

Mitzi Savrill lived in University and was beginning her master's degree. She was also chief cashier at

Grayson's. Although Soapy boasted of his close friendship with Mitzi, the redhead and Chip both knew where Mitzi's real interest centered. Chip Hilton was way out in front in that race!

When the teams ran out on the field to start the game, other spectators emerged from the parked cars and gathered behind the rope fence. The game officials, dressed and ready, walked out to the center of the field and gestured for the team captains to come forward. Chip and Biggie represented team A, and Ward and Hansen were the team B leaders. Ward won the toss and elected to receive. Chip chose to defend the east goal. The four players shook hands and hustled back to the sidelines to join in their team huddles.

Chip and his starting teammates were first to run out on the field for the kickoff. The team B players moved into receiving formation as Chip set the ball up on the kicking tee. He backtracked to his thirty-two-yard line and waited for the referee's signal. When the official blew the whistle, Chip started forward, picked up his teammates at the thirty-five-yard line, and booted the ball into the end zone. Miller had been standing on the goal line and scurried back for the ball. But when team A's front line raced past the thirty-yard line, he grounded the ball for the touchback.

The referee placed the ball on the twenty-yard line, checked the head linesman to make sure the chain was in place, and blasted his whistle. Back in his free-safety position, Chip checked his teammates. Whittemore, Cohen, Maxim, and Johnson made up the front four with Roberts, Aker, and McCarthy in the linebacker spots. Fireball was at right cornerback, his usual defensive position, and O'Malley was in the left cornerback position, opposite Hazzard.

O'Malley was out of position. He was a tackle but far too slow to cover speedy split ends. Chip moved closer to Speed. "O'Malley can't stay with Hazzard," he warned. "You cover the middle, and I'll drop back. OK?"

"Right!" Speed agreed.

Ward brought his team up to the line of scrimmage, barked his "Set! Hut! Hut! Hut!" and faked a handoff to Hansen. It was perfectly done, and the clever deception tricked the team A linebackers. They converged on the center of the line, and Ward hustled back several steps and got set for a pass. The fake helped Ward's receivers and gave them more time to run their patterns, which placed a heavy burden on the team A secondary. Kerr, Williams, and Hazzard were streaking down the field.

Chip checked his defensive teammates and watched Hazzard at the same time. Kerr was running directly toward Fireball, and the burly fullback was backtracking to keep the flankerback from getting behind him. O'Malley had retreated and was a short distance in front of Hazzard. Williams, team B's tight end, was cutting straight down the center of the field toward Speed.

"I have Williams!" Speed shouted.

A quick glance toward Hazzard and O'Malley convinced Chip that there would soon be nothing but daylight between the speeding end and the goal line. O'Malley was rapidly losing ground. Without further hesitation, Chip ambled back toward the left corner of the field.

Hazzard had been Ward's favorite receiver for two years. The tall end could stretch his long legs into a sprint that enabled him to run the hundred in nine and a half seconds in full uniform. In addition to his speed, the rangy end had the leap and the timing to go up and come down with the ball even when he was surrounded by opponents.

Ward had cocked his arm and was concentrating on Hazzard. He seemed about to release the ball, and

Chip felt sure Hazzard was running a fly play. If he could get to the right spot in time, he could try for an interception. Heading for his left corner at full speed, he risked a glance over his shoulder to locate the ball.

At that precise moment, Ward sprinted out of the pocket. The wily quarterback still had the ball and he had fooled team A's entire secondary, including Chip, who could have kicked himself! A free-safety player was always the last to commit himself on a play.

Then Chip saw Hansen. The tall fullback had broken through the center of the line and was all alone, sprinting for team A's right corner. Smart! Ward had used Hazzard, Kerr, and Williams as decoys and was scrambling to give Hansen time to break into the open. Chip swung his head around just as Williams ran a down-and-out with Speed in hot pursuit. Fireball had picked up Kerr and that left Hansen all alone, wide open, a perfect target for the bomb.

Chip whipped around in a tight circle and headed for the opposite corner of the field just as Ward released the ball. Fifteen yards more and Hansen took the ball over his shoulder. Without breaking stride, he streaked along the sideline, heading for the goal line. Now it was a race between Chip and the speeding fullback. Chip called on every ounce of his reserve strength and reached tackling distance at the ten-yard line. Leaving his feet in a desperate dive, he knocked Hansen out-of-bounds on the five.

The referee brought the ball in from out-of-bounds, and Chip called for a time-out. His teammates came trotting up and circled him in the huddle. "My fault," Chip said quickly.

"Wrong," Speed dissented. "Williams suckered me on a down-and-out."

"Forget it!" Biggie said roughly. "Let's stack our defense and get that ball." He poked a finger in

McCarthy's chest. "You key on Hansen and forget everyone else. You hear?"

"Count on it!" McCarthy growled.

Biggie was right. Ward fed the ball to Hansen up the middle and McCarthy, Cohen, and Maxim met him at the line of scrimmage and hurled him five yards back. The referee returned the ball to the five-yard line, and now it was second down and goal to go. Ward now faked a pitchout to Miller and sent Hansen over left tackle. That was a big mistake. Whittemore and Cohen broke through the line and wrestled Hansen to the ground on the seven-yard line. Now it was third and goal from the seven.

"Ward will pass to Hazzard," Cohen said in the huddle.

"Right," Chip agreed. "I'll back up O'Malley. Speed, you cover the middle. Fireball takes Kerr. Roberts, you cover Williams."

Cohen elbowed Whittemore. "Drive Williams back, Whitty. I'll handle the hole in the line."

Sure enough, just as Biggie had figured, Ward tried a pass to Hazzard. O'Malley kept between him and the corner, and Chip drove in from the middle and knocked the ball out-of-bounds.

Ward called a time-out.

In the team A huddle, Biggie looked to Chip for help. "You call it," he said.

"I think Ward will try Hazzard once more," Chip said confidently. "Run Williams back again, Whitty. Roberts, you play him if he gets away from Whitty. McCarthy, you zone the hole over center. Fireball takes Kerr. O'Malley, you play outside of Hazzard and try to run him inside. Speed and I will double-team him as he cuts for the goal post. Let's go!"

Ward faked to Hansen on a draw and then looked for Hazzard cutting down and in behind the right goal post. Hazzard got a step on O'Malley and cut right toward Chip. The pass was high, but Chip got to the ball a split second ahead of Hazzard and knocked it to the ground. It was team A's ball on its own seven-yard line, first and ten.

From that point on, it was team A all the way. Chip passed on the first down, hitting Whitty, his wide end, with a sideline pass. Whittemore carried to the twenty-four-yard line for a first down. Then, mixing the inside outside running of Fireball and Speed with flares and draws, Chip guided team A to team B's eight-yard line. With first down and goal to go, he sent Fireball over right guard. The hole closed, and Fireball changed directions. He followed Speed to the left and scored when his running mate threw the key block on Roth.

Chip kicked for the extra point, and it was 7-0.

Team B received, and Chip again kicked the ball into the end zone. With the ball on team B's twenty-yard line, Ward tried Hansen on two running plays that failed to get an inch. Then he hit Hazzard slanting across the middle for a first down on the thirty-eight-yard line. Hansen found an opening in the line and gained three yards. Ward tried another pass, but the blitz was on, and Whitty caught him from behind and dumped him for a loss of six yards.

It was third down and long yardage, and both teams knew the blitz was a must. Ward fell back in the pocket to pass, but he didn't have enough time. Maxim and Johnson opened a hole for McCarthy, and he and Fireball broke through the line. Hansen and Miller were bowled over as if they were tackling dummies, and Cohen hit Ward back on the eighteen-yard line with a crash that made Chip wince. But the little quarterback held on to the ball.

Now it was fourth down with thirty yards to go, and team B went into punt formation. Standing on his

six-yard line, Miller got a good punt away. The boot
carried to Morris on the midfield stripe. Chip took out
the first man down, and Speed was on his way, carrying the ball back to team B's twenty-nine. From that
point, team A scored in three plays.

Chip faked a pass, and Soapy and Anderson combined on a trap that permitted Hansen to break
through the middle of the line. Then they dumped him
from the side. Fireball took the ball from Chip and cut
past Hansen on the draw play, carrying the ball to the
eighteen-yard line for the first down.

Team B was blitzing now, and Chip hit Speed on a
screen pass that was good for six yards. Then, on a
rollout behind Anderson, Chip went over for the score.
He kicked the extra point and that made the score
team A 14, team B 0.

Ward elected to receive, but it was the same story
all over again. Team B couldn't gain, although Hansen
fought for every inch when he carried the ball. When
his team was on the defense, he keyed on Fireball. But
his front four gave him little help, and he had to give
ground time after time. As team A continued to pile up
the first downs, Hansen began to lash out at his defensive teammates with caustic fury. Nothing helped.
Team A had the superior blocking, and Fireball and
Speed romped through and around the team B line
almost at will.

Chip felt sorry for Hansen, but none of his teammates shared the feeling. Most of them had a score or
two to settle with the sullen fullback and had looked
forward to this day. Now they had their chance, and
they piled it on. Chip was glad to see, however, that
Greg Hansen could take it as well as give it. He was in
on every play and fought back with furious abandon.

As the game wore on, Chip knew that inwardly, if
not outwardly, a feeling of respect for the frustrated

fullback was building up in the heart of every member of team A. The slaughter was no fun and everyone was glad when the game ended. The score: team A 38, team B 0.

As soon as the timekeeper's whistle ended the game, Chip made a break for Hansen. The furious, fiery fullback had proved himself that afternoon. Hansen had taken everything thrown at him and come back fighting for more. That was the kind of player Chip Hilton wanted on *his* team and the kind of person he wanted as a friend.

Chip wasn't alone. Soapy, Fireball, Biggie, and Speed followed and joined him in shaking Hansen's hand and patting him on the back. Now, Chip noticed, Hansen grudgingly accepted Fireball's handshake.

Slow as it seemed, he *was* making progress with Hansen. Then Chip thought of the short time that remained before the first game, and his spirits fell. Coming up next week there would be classes and Soapy's morning study hour and his job and football practices and quarterback sessions with Ralston. On top of all that, there was Hansen. It would take a miracle to bring the grim, determined fullback around in a week. Maybe football wasn't worth all the setbacks and rebuffs a player met and all the sacrifices he had to make.

Then he thought of his mother back in Valley Falls and all the sacrifices she had made since the death of his father—how she had worked long hours as a telephone supervisor to keep their little family home going. Her greatest hope was that he would graduate from State, following in the footsteps of his father, Big Chip Hilton.

That did it! He lifted his head high and forced himself to quit feeling sorry for himself and to quit looking over his shoulder. No matter how many obstacles a person met, there was only one way he could go if his heart was right. And Chip's was. His priorities were firmly set. He had one option: straight ahead. He needed to be ready and willing to face up to life and whatever it had to offer, with a good attitude and trusting that Christ knew best. All Chip could do was be honest, work hard, and befriend Hansen.

CHAPTER 8

The Fastest Gun

THAT NIGHT, the players watched a film of the previous season's games. During the viewing, Coach Rockwell reversed the films for playbacks and to discuss certain situations. When the long day drew to an end, the coaches sent them back to their bunks to pack up for the next day's departure.

The next morning, after an early breakfast, Chip, Soapy, and Speed attended church services in the nearby town of Antlers. The three friends had visited the same church during each football training camp, and many people in the congregation remembered and greeted them warmly. Chip was always comforted knowing the church family had room for both familiar Christian brothers and sisters as well as newcomers.

Back at Camp Sundown, everyone joined in the general camp cleanup, and everything was shipshape by one o'clock. The cooks went all out for the final camp meal, serving New York strip, baked potatoes, corn on the cob, fresh garden salad, hot rolls, and apple pie à la mode. When the players could eat no more, Soapy hustled into the kitchen and escorted the entire kitchen staff into the dining room. Then the redhead led the players in a standing cheer of appreciation.

The buses arrived at three o'clock, and the players joyfully piled in for the two-hour ride to University. The first stop was Jefferson Hall. Chip, Soapy, Speed, Biggie, Whitty, Fireball, Anderson, and Maxim piled out. Collecting their luggage, they struggled down the marigold-lined walk, up the long stairs to the porch, and through the double front doors of the venerable brick dormitory.

The first-floor hall extended the length of the building. The doors along the broad hall led to lounges, study halls, Jeff's library, and the dorm's snack kitchen. Soapy was leading the way, but he stopped abruptly and dropped his bags noisily to the floor. "Look!" he cried, pointing toward the stairs leading to the second floor. "Look at that!"

His followers crowded forward and also paused in astonishment. Jeff's resident assistant, Pete Randolph, was sitting on a table in front of the stairway, swinging his long legs and smiling broadly. "Put them down," he said, waving toward the duffel bags and suitcases they were carrying.

"What is this?" Soapy demanded. "A sit-down strike?"

"No," Randolph said smugly, "just a little meeting to remind you fine gentlemen of the rules and regulations that govern this domicile."

"Here we go," Speed groaned, setting down his suitcase and leaning against the elevator door. "*Coach Randolph* wants to conduct a skull session."

"Bells!" Soapy shouted jubilantly. "You've got a new set of bells to play with."

"No new bells," Randolph said. "Just some new rules."

Everyone groaned, but Pete pulled a sheet of paper out of his pocket and read the building regulations slowly and loudly despite the protests of his residents. When he finished, he got off the table and carried the paper back to the bulletin board and waved toward the steps and the elevator. "Now, gentlemen," he said politely, "I hope you will cooperate so we can enjoy another pleasant year together. By the way, despite the privileges permitted in certain other dorms on State University's glorious campus, young ladies will *not* be permitted beyond the first floor of Jefferson Hall at anytime. Good night."

Soapy led the good-natured boos that followed Randolph's words, and then the guys trooped up the stairs. Chip and Soapy still shared room 212, Fireball and Biggie were now in room 214, and Speed, living alone, somehow had finessed his way into the largest room on the floor, room 216, at the end of the hall. The rest of the athletes lived in rooms on the third floor.

Chip and Soapy put their things away, stopped to get Fireball, and together took the shortcut across campus to Main Street and University's chief shopping center. When they reached Grayson's, Mitzi Savrill was in the cashier's booth just inside the main door. She smiled and welcomed them back. Soapy suddenly collapsed against Fireball.

"What's the matter with you?" Fireball asked, his voice filled with alarm.

"It's Mitzi," Soapy groaned, dramatically batting his eyelids. "I get a lump in my throat every time she looks at me."

"You're going to get a lump on your head if you pull that stunt again," Fireball said, grinning. "C'mon, let's get to work."

Chip and Mitzi talked for a minute or so, and then Chip went on back to the stockroom. He entered without knocking and found his stockroom assistant, Isaiah Redding, sitting at the desk.

Isaiah leaped to his feet. "Chip!" he cried. "Am I glad to see *you!* Now we'll have some records around here to check out."

It was a busy evening for Chip, but he took it in stride. Grayson's was the most popular spot in town for students and townspeople alike. The store had begun years ago as a small family pharmacy, but George Grayson had developed his business into one of the largest in the state. In addition to its extensive pharmacy, Grayson's sold just about everything, from novelties to plants to candles to small electronics to toys. In fact, the residents of University liked to say, "If Grayson's doesn't have it, you really don't need it!"

Of course, the big attractions for the college students were the food court and fountain area, complete with a big screen TV, a juke box, and several video game machines. The high school and college students gathered in front of the big screen TV to watch sporting events, and young families loved to drop in to treat their kids to burgers and ice cream at the old-fashioned soda fountain. Soapy was the big attraction for the high school students. He was as fast with his ice cream scoop as he was with a way-out story or a quick comeback to a wisecrack.

At eleven o'clock, Mitzi hung the "Sorry, But We're Closed" sign on the doors, and fifteen minutes later, Chip, Soapy, and Fireball were at Pete's Place, their favorite after-work hangout. They received a big reception from the owner, employees, and customers. After hamburgers, fries, and milk shakes, Chip and his pals left for Jeff.

Soapy's alarm clock blasted them from sleep at exactly 6:30 the next morning. The redhead leaped from his bed and began to pull on his sweats. Chip had been sound asleep. He raised himself on one elbow and glanced at the clock. "What goes?" he demanded.

"I'm getting into shape for our study hall program," Soapy said brightly.

"You've got to be kidding."

"Not at all. You guys voted it in last year, and the order still stands."

Chip groaned and turned his back to his determined roommate. Soapy's study hall program meant that Chip and his pals would start their study period Tuesday morning.

He turned back over to catch a few more minutes of shut-eye, but Soapy had done it again! Chip was wide awake. He showered and had just finished dressing when Soapy bounded back into the room with a box of doughnuts and two hot chocolates from the convenience store down the street. Later, he and Soapy walked across the campus to the Academic Services office and picked up their class schedules. Then they visited with old friends in the student union until it was time for lunch.

That afternoon, when Chip reported for practice, the final player list was posted on the bulletin board. He passed it by and continued to the equipment room where Murph Kelly was supervising the issue of varsity uniforms. He gathered his jersey and the rest of his gear and carried it up to the equipment room to store it in his locker. Then he dressed and went out on the field.

That afternoon and during the practices the rest of the week, coaches and players alike were looking ahead to the opening game of the season. The starting offensive and defensive units were set except for one or two spots. Hansen was a fixture on the defensive team as the middle linebacker, but Ralston was trying several players at the right guard on the offensive unit.

Chip continued his efforts to win Greg Hansen's confidence, but the fullback was still bitter and aloof. Chip didn't give up, and on Friday he got a break when he least expected it. He was on his way to Ralston's pregame quarterback session when he met Hansen.

The big player was also scheduled to attend the meeting, and they walked along together.

Hansen was reluctant to talk, but when Chip told him how much his work as the middle linebacker had improved the team defense, Hansen flared up. "I'll play there, of course," he said shortly. "But I'd better get a chance to play fullback a part of the game at Eastern."

Chip ignored the reference to the Eastern game. "Fireball will graduate in June, and you'll be a cinch to make fullback next year," he said.

"Without game experience this year?" Hansen cried. "You're out of your mind. Why, Ralston will have his *next* year's team picked before we play our last game *this* year. No way. I'm going to keep trying and hoping, and I'll be ready when my chance comes. You wait and see. I'll get a chance *this* year."

"But you don't know the fullback plays."

"I know the plays as well as Finley does. I practice them in the evenings and every Sunday with the high school kids."

It was the first time Chip had gotten Hansen to talk freely for a long time, and he wasn't going to waste the opportunity. "I don't see how they can help you," he said skeptically. "They sure can't know the plays—"

"What are you doing Sunday afternoon?" Hansen asked abruptly.

"Nothing. I'm free until after six o'clock. Then I have to go to work."

"All right. How about coming to my house around two o'clock for dinner?"

"Sure, thanks. But what's that got to do with the plays?"

"You'll find out when you meet the high school kids."

"I'll be there."

Hansen gave Chip his address, and Chip wrote it on the front page of his quarterback notebook. A few minutes later they reached the field house and made their way to the lecture room. Chip and Hansen were the last to report, and they had no more than taken their seats when Coach Ralston started the meeting.

"When I first took charge of State's football program," he said, "the first members of the squad I wanted to see were the quarterbacks and the middle linebackers. Among the four quarterbacks who reported was a sophomore from Valley Falls High School. He had played quarterback under Coach Rockwell. There were two fine middle linebackers on hand, the captain, Ace Gibbons, and his backup, Mel Osborn. Both were good, so I turned my attention to the quarterbacks.

"College coaches are a bit skeptical about extravagant stories concerning prep school athletes, especially when they come from small schools. However, in spring practice, Hilton proved he had all the assets of a good quarterback—the arm, the ballhandling techniques, the size, the intelligence, a good memory for plays and signals, and plenty of confidence. I knew right away he was my quarterback, and, although Chip was only a sophomore, I placed him in the number-one spot. Miller, Ward, what I am going to say about our quarterback requirements is for your benefit. Listen carefully.

"Quarterbacks must earn the respect of their teammates, on and off the field. If a quarterback cannot command respect from the players, he will never be the leader in whom they place their confidence. Hilton has mental confidence, and he has won the respect of his teammates and the coaching staff as well as college coaches throughout the country. They selected him to their first all-American offensive team, and the nation's sportswriters awarded him the Heisman trophy.

"Hilton gets rid of the ball faster than any quarter-back I have ever seen, and he can fake a throw while on the dead run." He smiled and added, "I suppose you might call him the *fastest gun* in college ranks.

"In our system, particularly in the split-T, we like to use rollouts and keepers to throw our opponent's front four off balance. Keep in mind that opponents who know a passer is always to be found in the pocket will pressure him all afternoon.

"Hilton is capable of rolling out or falling back in the pocket when he wants to pass. He is seldom forced to eat the ball, and I'm sure he set some kind of a college record last year because he attempted 176 passes without a single interception.

"When it comes to calling the plays, I'm not in favor of using guards to take plays in to the quarterback. There are times, of course, when we send in a play that our coaches think will be successful because of a weakness they spot in our opponent's defense.

"Time is the big factor in passing. That's the reason for the rush or blitz. If a quarterback had all the time he wanted to get the ball away, anyone could be a great passer. We give our passers all the protection possible, but they must be aware that they will be rushed, and they must accept the fact that they are going to get roughed up if they don't get rid of the ball.

"Now we come to signals. All of you know the numbers we use for our line holes and those we use for our plays. The 'Set! Hut! Hut!' we use for our starting signals are the best possible.

"Calling audibles at the line of scrimmage is necessary when the opponents have shifted into a formation that might stop a play. However, the first thing the quarterback must do in such situations is read the defense the opponents have set up. And he must do it in a hurry.

"The automatic call is used in about a third of the plays we call in the huddle. Our opponents have scouted us just as we have scouted them, so everything else being equal, the best tactician should win.

"A good quarterback can read the opponents' defensive alignments whether they are stunting or rolling or whether the front four are merely changing positions. Often a linebacker will jump into the line and a safety man will take his place. In such a situation, the quarterback must decide whether it's a fake or the real thing. You might call it multiple defensive reading.

"If the quarterback thinks the opponents are reading his audibles, he uses the colors we have worked out to change the assignment from one side of the line to the other. These colors are red, yellow, or green. And, if he wants to change the hole, he uses the colors we gave you yesterday: black, blue, or purple. As you know, these colors can be changed in the huddle—especially if the quarterback thinks the opponents are reading his calls."

Ralston ended his lecture and began to shoot questions at the various players. "How do you eat up the clock, Ward?"

"By keeping the ball on the ground and grinding out short gains, Coach."

"What methods can the quarterback use to help in this method?"

"Well, he can freeze the linebackers with fake handoffs to the backs and then roll out behind his line blockers."

"What about gambling situations, Miller?"

"If we're behind in the score and have the ball, we must decide whether to throw a pass or run a play. Especially when it's third down and we need a big gain. And, when we are in a kicking situation and need a big gain, we must decide whether to try a short kick, a rolling kick, or a medium kick that we might recover."

"What if the opponents have the ball and we're trying to run out the clock, Hansen?"

"We can stack the line and blitz their quarterback."

"Hilton, why does faking a throw help receivers?"

"It gives them more time to run their patterns."

"Ward, how do we use the sprintout?"

"We use it primarily as a run, Coach. But we can pass if one of our receivers breaks free."

"What do we mean by a movable pocket, Miller?"

"We set it up in the huddle, Coach. Our running backs use fake plunges and slants in order to reach the point where the quarterback wants the pocket."

"Hansen, what do we mean by a triple-stack of the line?"

"We move the secondary up close to the ball and place our linebackers directly behind linemen."

"What about the ends in this stack, Ward?"

"They float to the outside, Coach."

"Why do we use the double-wing formation, Miller?"

"To get a one-on-one or man-to-man passing situation."

"Hilton, what is the most important down?"

"The third down."

"Why?"

"Because that's the down when quarterbacks most often get caught with long yardage to go for a first down. They have to decide whether to run the ball or pass."

"There's a saying in football that the quarterback who can complete third-down plays consistently can kill any team. What does that mean, Ward?"

"Well, Coach, that's about the same thing Chip said. It means a team is dangerous anytime they have the ball, anyplace on the field, and on any play. A quarterback who can do that discourages a team that fights its heart out on the first two downs."

There was a clatter of footsteps in the hall outside. The steps slowed down just outside the door and a second later, Rockwell entered the room. "Excuse me, Coach. You said to have the rest of the players here at four o'clock to review the game plan. We're ready."

"Bring them in."

The players entered and found seats. Then Coaches Rockwell and Sullivan went over the offensive and defensive game plans for the next day. As this was a review of the plans made for Brandon, the coaches made the session as brief as possible. When they finished, Ralston excused the players with instructions to get a good night's rest and to report to Murph Kelly for bandaging and suiting-up at 11:30.

On the way out, Hansen caught up with Chip. "That night we were talking at the lake, why didn't you tell me you had won the Heisman Award?" he asked.

"I didn't think it was the right time," Chip said, smiling.

"It sure wasn't," Hansen agreed ruefully. "Don't forget Sunday."

"Don't worry," Chip assured him. "I'll be there."

He wasn't about to forget *that* invitation. Come Sunday night, he might know the answers to a lot of things behind Hansen's stubborn attitude.

An Empty Victory

THE CLOCK displayed 11:30 when Chip reached the
locker room. Not leaving anything to chance, Murph
Kelly personally taped his ankles. Then Chip went into
the locker room and put on his game uniform. The
white State University home jersey was trimmed with
red, the pants were blue with a white stripe running
down the sides, the socks were white, and the helmet
was white with a blue stripe running across the top
from front to back. He was dressed by 12:00 and, carrying his helmet, walked slowly along the hall to the
lecture room.

At the door, he glanced quickly at the whiteboard.
The starting offensive team was listed on the left side
of the board, and the names of the defensive players
were on the right.

AN EMPTY VICTORY

OFFENSIVE TEAM		DEFENSIVE TEAM	
Tight End	Montague	Left End	Whittemore
Left Tackle	Cohen	Left Tackle	Cohen
Left Guard	McCarthy	Right Tackle	Maxim
Center	Smith	Right End	O'Malley
Right Guard	Anderson	R Linebacker	Roberts
Right Tackle	Hazzard	L Linebacker	Aker
Quarterback	Hilton	L Cornerback	Johnson
Flankerback	Jacobs	Strong Safety	Miller
Running Back	Morris	R Cornerback	Finley
Running Back	Finley	Free Safety	Ward

Chip checked the offensive team first. He was the starting quarterback. A quick glance at the defensive unit showed that Ward and Miller were listed for the safety positions. Hansen was in the middle linebacker spot. Coach Ralston and his assistants arrived before Chip had finished his study of the two teams. Murph Kelly and Billy Joe Evans, the student bench manager, waited at the door.

Ralston glanced at his watch. "Twelve forty-five," he said. "Right on time. Take 'em out, Nelson, Stewart. Be back here at 1:30 sharp."

Chip led the players out of the room and along the alley to the players' exit, and then onto the field. After the group calisthenics, the players separated and went through their sprinting, kicking, and passing drills. Then the coaches herded them off the field and back to the lecture room. The clock showed 1:25.

Ralston waited for them to quiet. "Well, men," he said, a slight smile crossing his lips, "this is it! Murph Kelly says you're physically fit, and the coaches tell me you are mentally sharp and ready. Chip, Hansen, the two of you go out for the toss. If you win, receive. If not, defend the north goal. Wear your helmets when you run out on the field. We came to play."

Chip glanced at the stands when he ran through the exit and onto the field. Only a fraction of the seats were filled around the stadium, but he was thrilled by the reception from the student sections. Against the smattering of fans here and there, the student sections burst forward in a solid mass of red and white, like some exotic flower caught in bloom. The noise was deafening! In the middle of the field, the State University Marching Band formed precise lines, alternating between red and white. The sun flashed off the brass instruments, and the strains of State's Fight Song filling the air. The cheerleaders were leading their "Go! Go! Go!" cheer. Chip's spirits soared.

When both teams had reached their benches, the officials gathered in the center of the field. Chip and Hansen trotted out for the pregame details. The Brandon quarterback and defensive captain joined the circle, and the referee made the introductions.

The Brandon quarterback won the toss and chose to kick. Chip said State would defend the north goal. Two minutes later, he and Speed were standing on the State goal line. The referee blew his whistle, and the Brandon kicker started forward and kicked the ball. It was a fairly high boot; Chip figured the ball would carry to the ten-yard line. He moved slowly forward and, as the ball began to drop, sprinted straight ahead, catching it on the dead run. Speed took the lead as Chip followed him into the center of the wedge.

Speed dumped the first opponent to break through. Chip sped through the hole and reached the thirty-four-yard line before the kicker met him head-on. It was a good runback. Chip grunted in satisfaction. State was off to a good start.

The Statesmen huddled, and Chip decided to pass right away. "Hazzard!" he said sharply. "Down-and-out, sideline pass. Monty on a right angle. Jacobs on a fly. On two, guys. Let's go!"

At the line of scrimmage, Chip looked around the defensive line and began his count. "Set!" he called. "Hut! Hut! Hut!"

His teammates broke on the second signal, and Chip dropped straight back between Speed and Fireball. The line held, giving Chip time to check his receivers. Jacobs was sprinting straight up the field, and Monty was cutting into the hole over center. Hazzard was dashing straight ahead as if on a fly when Chip faked a throw. Then, just as Hazzard angled toward the sideline, Chip released the pass. Flash was leading his opponent by five yards when he caught the pass. He was close to the sideline, but he threw a hard stop, pivoted back, and cut for the center of the field.

The strong safety had picked up Whittemore at the forty-five-yard line, but he turned now to help cover Hazzard. Following his pass, Chip noted Hazzard's stride and change of pace and shook his head in admiration. Then Flash suddenly lengthened his stride and sped away from the strong safety. The free safety angled in, made a desperate dive, and managed to knock Hazzard down on the Brandon forty-five-yard line.

On the next play, Chip sent Finley off tackle, and the fullback picked up four yards. It was second and six. Chip faked to Finley and handed off to Morris. Speed followed Fireball into the line, spotted an opening on his right, cut through it, and carried to the Brandon thirty-six. It was close to a first down, but the referee spread his hands the length of the ball.

With a foot to go and to the surprise of no one, Chip sent Fireball over left tackle. The line was stacked, but

Montague, Cohen, and McCarthy blasted a hole, and Fireball carried for seven yards. That made it first and ten on the Brandon twenty-nine-yard line.

Chip tried a pass to Montague on a quick slant behind the Brandon middle linebacker, but the visitors' strong safety came in fast and knocked it down.

It was second and ten.

Chip faked another pass and handed off to Finley on the draw. The hard-hitting fullback picked up four yards to make it third down with six to go.

In the huddle, Chip called for a keeper with Speed trailing for a lateral. Taking the ball from Soapy, Chip sprinted out to his right. Anderson shunted the left linebacker aside, and McCarthy decked the left corner with a cross-body block that put Chip in the clear. Driving along the sideline, he made it to the Brandon twelve-yard line for another first down.

In the huddle, he tagged Montague for an in-and-out end-zone corner pass. He faked to Fireball, who was driving into the line, and rolled out to his left behind Speed, McCarthy, and Anderson. Faking the throw as Monty turned in, Chip took three more strides and fired the ball toward the corner. Montague swerved to the outside, leaped high in the air, pulled in the ball, and landed just in bounds for the touchdown. Chip booted the extra point and State led, 7-0.

Brandon elected to receive, and Chip trotted back to the State forty-yard line. *It was too easy,* he told himself. *We'll slaughter them.* Curly Ralston sent in the rest of the kicking team, and Chip booted the ball down to Brandon's five-yard line. The receiver ran the ball back to the twenty-five where he was downed by Maxim. As soon as the runner hit the ground, Ward came racing in to replace Chip.

State's defensive weakness showed up right away. The Brandon quarterback avoided the Statesmen's front four—Whittemore, Cohen, Maxim, and O'Malley—and passed over them or ran the ends. When they blitzed, he hit his backs in the flat with flare passes. Brandon marched up the field to the State twenty-yard line. Then, Ralston called a time-out and sent Chip, Speed, and Jacobs in for Johnson, Miller, and Ward.

When time was in, the Brandon quarterback attempted a draw play. Hansen met the power back at the line of scrimmage for no gain. On second down, the quarterback attempted an end-zone pass that Chip knocked out-of-bounds. When State huddled, Hansen made the right call. "We rush," he said. The blitzing front four, combined with Hansen, Aker, and Roberts right behind them, forced the quarterback to retreat. He was downed back on the State twenty-nine-yard line. As soon as he got to his feet, he called for a time-out.

The Brandon coach sent in his placekick team, and Hansen called for the ten-man rush. As Chip backed up to his solitary position in the secondary, he was thinking what a great game Hansen had played so far and how quickly he had taken charge of the Statesmen's defensive team.

On the pass from center, the Brandon line came apart. Whittemore, Cohen, and Aker were the first to penetrate and they combined to block the kick. Finley fell on the ball on the State thirty-yard line. The quarter ended before State got out of the huddle and the teams exchanged goals. Chip took charge once more and, accompanied by the thundering "Go! Go! Go!" from the stands, led State to a touchdown in nine plays. He kicked the extra point, making the score State 14, Brandon 0.

Brandon received and, using the same tactics that had worked before, advanced to State's thirty-yard line. Then the quarterback faked a pass and used his fullback on a draw play. Hansen had led the blitz, and the fullback found a hole right in the middle of the State line. He dashed straight up the middle. Miller was in the strong-safety spot, but the visitors' right end flattened him. The ball carrier made it to the State three-yard line before he was downed by Ward.

Sullivan gave the signal for a time-out, and Hansen called it. Then Ralston replaced O'Malley, Roberts, Miller, and Ward with Montague, McCarthy, Speed, and Chip. Now State's defense stiffened and held. Speed and Chip covered the middle and knocked down two passes, and Montague cut in front of Brandon's right end and dropped the ball carrier for a five-yard loss. On the fourth down Brandon tried another place-kick. Hansen called for the ten-man rush once again, and Cohen broke through to block the kick. Montague fell on the ball on State's thirty-yard line.

Ralston then sent in a backfield composed of Ward, Miller, Aker, and Roberts. Ward hit Hazzard on the first play for a forty-yard gain and gave the ball to Aker on a sweep that carried to the Brandon fifteen-yard line. The visitors called for a time-out.

When play was resumed, Ward hit Hazzard again. Flash took the ball on the Brandon five and sprinted across the goal line for the touchdown. Ralston sent Chip in for Ward and Speed for Miller, and the place-kick specialists combined for a perfect placement and the extra point. The score: State 21, Brandon 0.

Brandon elected to receive once more, and Chip kicked the ball into the end zone. The receiver grounded the ball for the touchback, and Ralston sent in his original defensive unit. Brandon began another march and advanced to the State forty-yard line before Ralston again changed his defensive team lineup. Now State held, and the Brandon kicker punted out-of-bounds on the State five-yard line. Before State could put the ball in play, the half ended.

The second half was more of the same. Except for kicking three extra points with Speed holding the ball, Chip and Morris sat out the entire half. Brandon had lost its pep and fight, and State's defensive team managed to hold the visitors scoreless. But Ward, Miller, Finley, and Jacobs had a field day, scoring three more touchdowns. The final score: State 42, Brandon 0.

Many of the fans left in the third quarter, but those who remained to the end were rewarded. Ward and Hazzard combined to complete a sensational sixty-five-yard touchdown pass. It had been a runaway game, and as Chip walked along with Speed and Soapy, he couldn't help thinking that it had been a wasted afternoon. Ralston hadn't learned much about his defense today.

Greg Hansen trotted up beside Chip at that moment. "Now what do you think of Ward?" he demanded.

"I think he's good," Chip said. "I always did."

"You ever see a better passing show than the one he put on in the second half?" Hansen persisted.

"Don't think so."

"There's no reason why Ralston couldn't have used me at fullback in that last half."

"You played the entire half on defense. Perhaps Coach doesn't think you know the fullback plays."

"Wait until tomorrow afternoon," Hansen said grimly. "I'll show you I know them. A couple of other things too!"

"I'll be there," Chip assured him.

Greg caught sight of Ward up ahead and continued on at a trot. "See you tomorrow," he called back over his shoulder.

"What's that all about?" Soapy asked.

"He invited me to his house for dinner."

"You're kidding!" Soapy said.

"What do you know about that?" Speed added. "How come the sudden turn to palsy-walsy?"

"Just one of those things," Chip said. "Come on, Soapy. We're due at Grayson's right away. With this victory, there'll be a big crowd there tonight."

When they reached the locker room, the State players had already begun celebrating their first win of the season. Chip, Soapy, and Fireball passed it up. They had no time for fun.

Chip was thinking that, as far as he was concerned, it had been an empty victory. Brandon had been woefully weak, and there wasn't much fun in celebrating a pushover win.

Saturday was always a busy day at Grayson's. And after a home game, particularly a win, the store was jammed. Chip and his pals quickly changed into their work uniforms and were on the job almost as soon as the fans arrived. The fountain was crowded three deep when Soapy and Fireball went to work behind the counter.

Chip went on back to the storeroom and found Isaiah struggling with a flood of orders. It was eleven o'clock before they caught up and nearly midnight when Chip and his pals reached Jeff. Soapy joined a bull session in the dormitory snack kitchen, but Chip went on upstairs and dressed for bed. It had been a long day with nothing much to feel good about. Maybe tomorrow would be different.

CHAPTER 10

Soccer-Style Kicker

CHIP LOCATED Nanford Avenue, the street on which the Hansen family lived, and checked the house numbers until he came to 12505. The Hansen home was a two-story red brick house separated from the sidewalk by a low picket fence and a small, neatly kept lawn with the largest marigolds Chip had ever seen. Chip walked up on the porch and was about to lift the brass knocker when Greg opened the door.

"I'm glad you came," Greg said. "Come on in. I want you to meet my dad."

Greg ushered Chip into a room just off the entrance hall. The room was small, but the strongly built man who was sitting beside the window in a wheelchair made it seem even smaller. He had been reading a newspaper. Now he dropped it in his lap and waited for Greg's introduction.

"Dad," Greg said, "this is Chip Hilton."

The big man managed a brief smile and acknowledged the introduction, but then his face fell expressionless. Chip extended his hand and was surprised by the strength, size, and thickness of Mr. Hansen's hand. Chip had a big hand and long fingers, but this man's hand dwarfed his as though it was that of a child. "Glad to meet you, Hilton," Mr. Hansen said briefly. "Make yourself at home."

There was an aloofness in Mr. Hansen's manner that left Chip feeling awkward. He felt completely out of place and was relieved when Greg gestured toward the hall. "Mom's in the kitchen," he said quickly. "Let's go back and you can meet her."

They walked down the hall, passed a small dining room, and came into an even smaller kitchen. A short, slight woman was busy at the stove when they entered. "Mother," Greg called softly, "Chip Hilton is here."

Mrs. Hansen turned quickly away from the stove and walked toward Chip. Her short hair was light brown, and the blue eyes smiling at him were warm and friendly. "I am happy to meet you, Mr. Hilton. Greg has spoken often of you." Her voice was low and warm, and the hand she held out for Chip's grasp was firm, yet gentle.

"Just call me Chip, Mrs. Hansen."

"Chip it is," she said, smiling. "Greg, I know the high school boys will be waiting anxiously to meet your guest, so you can leave right after dinner."

"What about the dishes?"

"I'll take care of them. I already have a lot of the pots and pans out of the way. No, you go ahead. Dinner will be ready in just a few minutes. Why don't you show Chip our garden?"

"You mean *your* garden!" Greg retorted fondly. "Come on, Chip. Her mind is made up."

Chip followed Greg out the back door and stopped on the porch in surprise. He had been amazed at the marigolds in the front, but this! The entire yard was covered with a breathtaking mass of colors, a display of beauty. Chrysanthemums, dahlias, gladiolas, and crepe myrtles in colors ranging from pure whites to deep reds, yellows, and soft pinks were at the height of their blooming. "Wow!" Chip exclaimed. "Your mother must spend *all* her time out here."

"Just evenings and Saturdays," Greg said. "She doesn't get home from work until nearly six o'clock."

"It's beautiful."

"Yes, it is," Greg agreed quietly. "The garden reflects my mother's beauty and her love for beautiful things."

This was an insight into a part of Hansen that Chip had been looking for, and he pondered the discovery keenly. The hard-nosed fullback *did* have a softness under the tough veneer he kept on the surface. Coupled with the contrast between Mr. Hansen's abruptness and Mrs. Hansen's warm greeting, this discovery meant something important.

It was clear that Mrs. Hansen was glad Greg and Chip were friends. Mr. Hansen was a different story. He had barely acknowledged the introduction. At any rate, Chip felt that the answer to Greg's football behavior was not far removed from this house.

A few minutes later, Mrs. Hansen called to them from the back window of the kitchen and announced that dinner was ready. Greg led the way back through the house and into the dining room. The table was tastefully arranged with a large vase of flowers as the centerpiece. Mr. Hansen was sitting in his wheelchair at the head of the table. Mrs. Hansen was waiting behind a chair on the side of the table nearest the kitchen.

"You sit there, Chip," she said, "opposite me."

Chip stood behind his chair while Greg walked behind his mother and held her chair until she was seated. Then he took his place at the end of the table opposite his father.

As soon as Greg sat down, Mr. Hansen said grace, and then Mrs. Hansen began to fill each of their plates. Mrs. Hansen served Chip first, then Mr. Hansen, then Greg, and herself last. There was plenty to eat—roast beef, mashed potatoes, brown gravy, green beans, fruit salad, and rolls and butter.

Greg and Chip wasted no time. Both were hungry and enjoyed the meal. But, as much as he enjoyed the food, Chip could not help but observe the attention that Greg gave to Mr. Hansen. Chip sensed that Greg loved his mother, but it was obvious that he worshiped his father.

"Greg played a great defensive game yesterday, Mr. Hansen," Chip said.

There was a sudden silence. Mr. Hansen looked briefly toward Chip and nodded, his face devoid of interest. Then he continued with his food.

Chip was embarrassed once again, but his words had apparently passed unnoticed by Greg and Mrs. Hansen. He decided right then to concentrate on eating and forget conversation.

When the main part of the dinner was finished, Mrs. Hansen announced that there was apple cobbler with ice cream for dessert. Mr. Hansen declined the dessert, excused himself, and propelled the wheelchair from the room. No one attempted to help him, but it was quite understandable. Chip had never seen broader shoulders or more heavily muscled arms on any man.

When he finished the cobbler and ice cream, Chip sighed and smiled at Mrs. Hansen. "I wish the student union served food like this. This is one meal I won't forget in a hurry. It was great! Are you sure we can't help with the dishes?"

"I'm sure," Mrs. Hansen said. "You boys run along. Be sure to come back again, Chip. You will always be welcome in our home."

Chip followed Greg back down the hallway and out on the porch to the street. Neither Mr. Hansen nor the wheelchair was in sight, and Chip surmised that Greg's father must be in an adjoining room.

Greg must have sensed Chip's thoughts. "Dad is in his study," he said quickly. "He spends most of his time there. The study is just off the front room and leads to his bedroom. My room is upstairs. I guess you noticed my father's reaction when you mentioned the football game."

Chip nodded. "Yes, I did. I hope it was OK for me to say that."

"I should have warned you," Greg said slowly, choosing his words carefully. "My father never talks about football. To me, my mother, or anyone else. He . . . well, I guess he just doesn't *like* the game."

"There are a lot of people like that," Chip said, feeling anxious to end the discussion.

Greg pointed to a large field at the end of the street. "There they are," he said proudly. "All the neighborhood kids and the high school players. They're waiting just for you. When I said you were coming, a lot of them thought I was kidding."

The field was swarming with young people, with many in nondescript football uniforms, some in T-shirts and jeans, and others in shorts and sweatshirts. They were passing and kicking footballs around, running and shouting, and obviously enjoying their informal workout. One of the younger boys spotted Greg and Chip and called out to the others. Immediately, all activity stopped. The boys came running up, eyeing and appraising Chip as they approached.

"Hiya, fellows," Greg said. "This is Chip Hilton, State's quarterback and captain. Why don't you step up here and shake hands with him?"

The boys crowded forward with one of the older boys leading the way. "My name is Carey," he said, extending his hand. "I play quarterback for University High School."

Chip shook hands with Carey and each boy who followed. When all of them had been through the line, Greg organized them by teams and they began to run plays. Then Greg moved into one of the running-back positions on Carey's team. "All right, Chip," he said, "you wanted to see if I knew State's fullback plays. Watch!"

Chip followed Carey's team and was surprised by the boys' knowledge and execution of State's plays. "They even use our signals," he whispered to himself. Then he concentrated on Greg. The big fellow ran fast, started quickly, and carried out the fullback assignments perfectly.

When they reached the end of the field, twenty yards or so in front of the homemade goal, Chip was surprised even more. Carey called for a placekick formation. Greg slipped out of his shoes. Then, with Carey holding the ball, Greg booted the ball soccer style. And, Chip noticed, with his left foot. Greg had tremendous leg power! The ball cleared the homemade uprights and landed far beyond them.

Several of the smaller youngsters were waiting beyond the goal and scrambled furiously for the ball. One of them snatched it up, came tearing back, and handed it to the center. Carey moved the formation back until the ball was approximately forty yards from the goal. Greg took his position and again booted the ball between the uprights.

"That's *real* kicking, Greg," Chip said. "I've watched the pro players kick placekicks soccer style, but I never saw anyone kick a football barefooted."

Greg grinned. "I know," he said. "I learned that playing soccer."

Carey turned the team around, and the youngsters started back up the field. After a few plays, Chip asked Carey if he could alternate with him at quarterback.

"Can you?" Carey said quickly. "And *how!"*

Chip alternated with the high school quarterback in calling the plays and handling the ball, and soon every youngster on the field was following the high school players and watching every move Chip made.

He was due at Grayson's at six o'clock and was genuinely sorry when it was time to leave. The players gathered around him, and Carey shook his hand and invited him back.

"I'll be back whenever I can make it," Chip promised. "I had a great time."

Greg walked along with him as far as the corner. They stopped for a moment to say good-bye, and Chip seized the opportunity to compliment Greg. "By the way," he said, "I take back what I said about you not knowing the fullback plays."

"Well, that's a start," Greg said grimly. "At least *you* know I'll be ready when my chance comes."

"Right!" Chip said. "And I mean it when I say that I hope Coach gives you a chance at fullback in a game. But don't misunderstand me. I still think Fireball is the best fullback in the country."

"I know," Hansen said impatiently. "Time will tell. See you at practice tomorrow."

Chip said good-bye and turned away. But his departure didn't mean that he had put the Hansen family out of his mind. All the way to Grayson's, he thought about them. Greg had said his father couldn't do physical work but that he did some writing and worked at home on his computer. Mrs. Hansen worked in one of the offices at State, and Greg did odd jobs when he could find them. There was one thing Chip knew now for sure. Greg Hansen was an entirely different person away from State's football team. Now, to find the reason. . . .

Chip reached the store a few minutes early and went directly to the stockroom. Sitting down at the desk, he listed the possible reasons for Mr. Hansen's lack of interest in Greg's football career.

Mr. Hansen:
1. Is bitter because of his physical disability.
2. Resents his inability to provide a living for his family.
3. Is disturbed because Mrs. Hansen must work.
4. Feels Greg should work instead of play football.
5. Believes football is a dangerous game.
6. Doesn't like sports.

Next, he listed the possible reasons for Greg's football attitude.

Greg Hansen:
1. Feels bad because he cannot help with family finances.
2. Wants to make his father proud of him. (Backs get lots of publicity; linemen do not.)
3. Is looking forward to a professional football career so he can help support his family.
4. Likes to play in the backfield.
5. Is disturbed by some personal problem.
6. Is obsessed with his personal infallibility.

SOCCER-STYLE KICKER

It wasn't much of start, but it was something. Chip felt that he had made a lot of progress today with Greg, but he wasn't satisfied. Mrs. Hansen might provide the best approach, especially since there didn't seem to be much hope that he would ever be able to break through Mr. Hansen's barrier. If he could find out something about Mr. Hansen's background, then Chip might discover the reason for his dislike for football.

Suddenly he had the answer. Greg had said his parents grew up in Eastern. Why not check into Mr. Hansen's background before or after the game with Eastern State?

CHAPTER 11

A Fullback Family

STATE UNIVERSITY'S easy victory over Brandon University meant a hard workout on Monday. Coach Ralston's practice philosophy never varied in that respect. A hard game on Saturday meant an easy practice in light gear on Monday, and an easy win meant a hard workout in heavy practice uniforms.

So, Monday afternoon, when the Statesmen reported to the field, they knew what was coming, and they were mentally and physically prepared for a hard defensive workout. Coach Ralston assembled them in the bleachers and immediately confirmed their expectations. "Brandon couldn't move the ball against a good high school team," he snapped. "But they moved it against us. That means our defense is inadequate, and if it does not improve between now and Saturday, Eastern will run us right out of their new stadium.

"Now for some details about the trip. We leave by bus at ten o'clock Friday morning. We will stay at the Eastern Sheraton Hotel Friday night and return to

University Saturday after the game. Coach Rockwell will be in his office tomorrow to issue letters from academic services to let your professors know we'll be on the road. Be sure you find out what classes you will miss and make arrangements with each professor. Remember, when we're not on the road, you are expected to attend *all* your classes. All right, let's go to work."

The next four days were blood days. Except for short periods devoted to a few offensive details, every minute of practice focused on team defense. As the days passed, it was clear that Ralston was satisfied with his front four. He had summarily placed Montague, the offensive unit's tight end, in the defensive right end position. This meant that Monty was going to have double duty and would play both ways.

It was a hard week for all of the players, but especially for Chip. The stockroom at Grayson's was still in bad shape and required a lot of attention. Course assignments were getting more demanding, and he had to fight to keep up. Despite the many demands on his time, he had continued to concentrate on Greg and the steps he might take while in Eastern to trace Mr. Hansen's background. He had tried an internet search on the Hansens, but that had come up cold.

He was at an impasse until Thursday morning. He and Soapy were in the Metcalf Library during a free period, doing some research, when, right out of the blue, it hit him. He wouldn't have much time to spend in Eastern, but what better place than in Eastern's public library?

"That's it!" he said jubilantly.

"What's it?" Soapy echoed.

"Just an idea I had."

Soapy leaned back in his chair and focused his blue eyes on Chip's face for a brief moment. "You're as bad

as Ralston," he snorted with disgust. "He's been keeping everyone off balance all week. I'll be glad when he
gets this Eastern game out of his system and you get
Hansen out of yours. Bah! You're both crazy. C'mon,
let's get something to eat."

Friday morning, the buses took off on schedule and
arrived in Eastern at 3:00. After getting settled in their
rooms at the Sheraton, the players again boarded the
buses to travel to one of Eastern's practice fields for a
light workout. They were back at the hotel at 6:30.
Following the team dinner, Kelly took them for a short
walk.

As usual, Coach Ralston had booked one of the
hotel's conference rooms for a review of the game plan.
All business, he covered the game notes briskly and
excused them just before nine o'clock. "Bed check at
eleven," he reminded them pointedly.

As soon as Ralston dismissed them, Chip bolted for
the door and managed to slip away from Soapy. The
library was only four blocks from the hotel, and he was
relieved to find that it did not close until ten o'clock.

An older woman was at the reception desk. Chip
asked her if it was possible to locate a former resident
through the library records. The receptionist shook her
head negatively. "No," she said courteously, "your best
source for that is the town hall. You could go through
the public records there. However, those offices won't
be open until Monday morning."

"I'm afraid that would be too late. I have to leave
Eastern tomorrow evening."

"If it's not too personal, would you mind telling me
who or what you're looking for? I've lived here a long
time, and perhaps I might be of some assistance."

Chip nodded. "Yes, perhaps you can help. I'm looking for some information concerning a man by the
name of Hansen. He grew up in Eastern."

"I see. Do you know his first name?"

Chip could have kicked himself. "No," he said ruefully, "I don't." He thought about it for a moment and then continued, "Mr. Hansen has a son by the name of Greg. Would that help?"

"I doubt it. However, if Mr. Hansen grew up in Eastern, he undoubtedly went to school here. How old would you say he is now?"

"Well, his son is twenty years old, so I guess Mr. Hansen would be in his forties."

"That might help. The graduating classes from the local high school are listed each year in the local newspapers. Let's start there. The newspaper morgue is downstairs. By the way, my name is Mrs. Grace White."

"Mine is William Hilton."

"I'm glad to know you, William. Now you wait right here until I get someone to cover the desk."

Mrs. White was back in a short time with a young man. He took her place behind the desk, and she led Chip down the wide steps to the basement. "This is it," she said, leading Chip into a large room on the left.

From floor to ceiling, the room was lined with shelves, all newspaper width and sorted by years. The shelves could be pulled out and rotated so that each month of each year could be located. A cross-index accompanied each month.

"All those?" Chip asked in despair, looking at his watch.

"Yes, William. But don't worry. We have microfilm indexes."

Miss White worked swiftly and surely with the microfilm. Starting with the June issues back some twenty-five years previously, she consulted each month. She stopped with the fifth tape and tapped the machine several times with a forefinger. "I think we have something," she said triumphantly. "At least we have found someone by the name of Hansen. You can read the article here on the microfiche, or would you prefer the actual paper?"

"Could I see the actual paper?" Chip asked.

She nodded, checked the film again, scribbled down a reference, and then pulled a newspaper from one of the shelves. She handed it to him. "Look in the sports section," she said. "Page 56."

Chip felt as if his fingers were all thumbs, but he finally found the page. The first thing he saw, at the top of the page, was a picture of a young man in a football uniform. He had broad shoulders, a thick neck, and a strong chin. Chip glanced quickly at the headline under the picture.

JOHN HANSEN
EASTERN'S ALL-STATE FULLBACK
LATEST ALL-STAR OF FAMILY
OF FULLBACKS

There was no doubt about it! The man in the picture was Mr. Hansen. He had changed during the years, of course, but the resemblance was unmistakable. Chip read the paragraph beneath the picture.

> John Hansen, Eastern High School's all-state star, will start at fullback for the West team in the all-American high school game. John III, the current representative of three generations of Hansen family fullbacks, will graduate next June and has been contacted by more than one hundred colleges with attractive athletic scholarship offers.

Chip paused and studied the young athlete's features. Greg bore little likeness to his father as a young man. For that matter, he mused, there was little resemblance between father and son even now. He continued reading the article.

> The father of John Hansen III starred for three years at Eastern High and was named to the all-state team just like the original John Hansen . . .

A chime rang out, the sound reverberating through the basement. Mrs. White confirmed that it was closing time. "We open at nine o'clock tomorrow morning," she said helpfully.

"I'll be busy all day tomorrow," Chip said regretfully. He thanked Mrs. White for her kindness and started back to the hotel. On the way, he reviewed the evening's revelations. Greg's behavior was now more understandable. As do most boys, Greg wanted desperately to follow in his father's footsteps. And his grandfather and his great-grandfather, too, Chip reflected.

Chip understood exactly how Greg felt. He had felt the same way about *his* father and still did. William Hilton Senior had excelled as a chemistry student and achieved all-American status playing three varsity sports at State University. And Chip had managed to do the same thing. Still, he mused, there was something decidedly wrong about Greg and Mr. Hansen.

Mr. Hansen had been an all-American high school player, yet he had turned against football. And, apparently, he had no interest in Greg's football career. That just didn't make sense. It was obvious that Mr. Hansen had suffered a serious injury. Perhaps he had been in an automobile accident. Or perhaps he had been injured on his job. Or in professional football? He had been big enough and good enough as a high school player to have developed into a college and professional star. If he had been injured in college or pro ball, that also might account for his dislike for football.

Anyway, Chip reflected, he now knew why Greg was adamant about securing a fullback position. Greg was determined to play the same position his father and his father's forefathers had played, and it was going to take some doing to change *that* ambition. Nevertheless, Chip was thinking, there had to be some way to win Greg over.

The team's only offensive weakness was at the right-guard position. Anderson was fast and quick and had played well in the left-guard position the previous year, but there was no one who could fill the right-guard position efficiently. All the players Ralston had tried could block well enough, but they were far too slow to be of much help on a sprintout or a running pass.

Chip liked to run to the right. Moving to the left to reach a passing pocket was all right, but on a keeper or running-pass play to the left, he was at a disadvantage. Besides, Jackknife Jacobs was a good lefty passer and the left-right passing combination opened up opponents' defensive alignments.

So, Chip concluded, if Hansen was the only player on the squad who could give State a complete offense, Chip Hilton wasn't giving up until that move had been accomplished!

Within just a few minutes, Chip was back at the hotel and riding the elevator to the tenth floor. The room he was sharing with Soapy was right down the hall from the elevator. He inserted the magnetic key card and swung the door open to find Soapy sprawled out on one of the beds, remote in hand, watching a sitcom on TV. On the table in the corner, Chip noticed the remnants of room service. A hot fudge sundae, now a melted glob of brown and white with a wilted cherry on top, seemed to stare at him accusingly.

"Where did you go?" Soapy asked indignantly. "I looked *everywhere* for you."

"I went to the library."

"The library? What for?"

"I had to look up something."

"I got you some ice cream, but I don't think it's good anymore."

"Sorry, Soapy," Chip said. "I should have told you I'd be gone awhile."

"Did you see any of the Eastern papers at the library?" Soapy asked, seeming to have forgotten about the sundae.

"No, I didn't. Why?"

"Both of them picked Eastern by three touchdowns. The evening paper said the only good thing about the game was the experience the benchwarmers would gain. What do you think about that?"

"I think games are won on the field. Besides, you shouldn't believe everything you read in the papers."

"I don't. The only thing I believe is what I see on the scoreboard after a game is over."

Chip was thinking about his next step and nodded absentmindedly. "Me too. Hey, Soapy, do you think you can get Biggie and Speed and Fireball in here?"

"Sure!" Soapy said. He leaped to his feet and picked up the phone on the table between the two beds. "I'll just call the front desk."

"You don't have to call the desk, Soapy. Just dial the rooms direct."

The red head grinned and shook his head. With a flourish, he punched zero. "Hello, is this Ms. Garcia at the front desk? This is Soapy Smith," he said casually. "You know, State's all-American football star—

"An autograph? Why sure! Anytime! Right now, however, I'd like for you to summon some of my teammates to my room for a conference. Mr. Cohen and Mr. Morris in room 1012 and Mr. Finley in room 1014.

"Yes, they are all on this floor. By the way, please hurry. It's important. It has something to do with my strategy for tomorrow's game. Say! You don't suppose this room could be bugged do you?

"No, not bedbugs. I mean wiretapped."

"No! Oh, thanks. That's good. Now, what time do you finish work?"

"Eleven o'clock bed check," Chip warned in a whisper, trying to conceal his grin.

Soapy placed a hand over the mouthpiece. "I know, I know," he mouthed. He removed his hand and continued. "Oh, that's too bad, and it's too late. Coach tucks me in at eleven o'clock, you know. If I wasn't on an upset tomorrow—Oh, well, some other time.

"The autograph? Of course. You come right down to the field after the game and as soon as my teammates let me down off their shoulders, I'll sign a dozen programs. All for you. Bye now."

Five minutes later, Biggie, Speed, and Fireball knocked on the door and barged into the room. "What's up?" Biggie asked.

"Something confidential," Chip said. "Sit down for a couple of minutes."

As soon as they found places to sit, he continued. "I've found out some things about Hansen that explain why he has been acting so unreasonably—"

"Wonders never cease," Soapy observed.

"It's something that makes a lot of sense, but it's also personal," Chip explained. "And it could happen to any of us. He needs our understanding, guys. I don't feel that I can ethically reveal what I know right now, but I am asking all of you to accept my word for it."

"That's good enough for me," Biggie declared decisively.

"Right!" the others chorused.

"Anything else?" Fireball asked.

"Yes, there is. I want you to give him a lot of encouragement tomorrow. Pat him on the back when he makes a good play and make a fuss over him generally. Eastern is a big test for all of us, but it's probably more important to him than any game he'll ever play. OK?"

Speed, Biggie, and Fireball nodded, but Soapy came up with the words. "Are you kidding?" he asked. "Of course it's OK! Er, let's see now—"

Soapy hopped up on his bed and began rapping, "We slap Hansen on the back, and put Eastern on the rack. We pat Hansen on the cheek, and break Eastern's two-year streak."

He paused and looked around triumphantly. "Pretty tight, eh?"

"Just don't quit your day job, man," Speed drawled.

CHAPTER 12

Giant Middleman

CURLY RALSTON had advised his players time and again that the wind was the most important weather element in the game of football. Yes, the wind. Some of the players had debated the matter with the veteran coach since many felt that a muddy or frozen field was more of a factor to the game's outcome. But Chip had never questioned Ralston's opinion. He knew that with the wind at his back, the player kicking off, punting, or placekicking had a terrific advantage. The same thing held true for passers and runners.

That was the reason he was standing on the State thirty-three-yard line with the wind pressing against his back. He had won the toss and chosen to defend the south goal. The Eastern captain had elected to receive. Chip glanced along the thirty-five-yard line where State's kicking team was waiting for the referee's whistle. Hansen, Maxim, McCarthy, Montague, and Aker were to his left, in that order. Cohen, O'Malley, Finley,

Miller, and Whittemore were to his right. It was the best kickoff team State could field.

The referee raised his arm, and the Eastern captain returned the signal. It was now or never! Chip started slowly forward and drove his foot into the perfect spot on the ball for a high kick. The ball rose sharply, caught by the wind, and sailed over the goal line and through the goal posts, landing beyond the running track that circled the field, far out-of-bounds. It was a mighty boot, and a roar emanated from the stands.

The referee trotted out to the Eastern twenty and gave the signal for the game clock to start. Chip followed his kick only a few yards because Whip Ward was racing in to replace him in the free-safety position. When Chip reached the bench, Ralston slapped him on the back without shifting his eyes from the field. "Nice kick, Hilton," he said.

Murph Kelly slipped a blanket over his shoulders, and Chip sat down beside Speed. But he leaped to his feet when the Eastern quarterback passed the ball on the first down. The flankerback on the left side of the field and the tight end were cutting directly toward State's safety backs, Ward and Miller. Both Eastern receivers were tall and fast, and Chip could see the play coming.

Ward, at five-nine, was far too short to cope with a six-four receiver. Miller had picked up the flankerback who had cut past Aker, and it was up to Ward to defend the taller tight end. The passer barely had time to get the ball away, but he managed to fire it toward the end. The tall receiver went high above Ward, caught the ball with his fingertips, and landed running.

Miller had left the flankerback as soon as the passer released the ball, and he downed the big end on the Eastern forty-yard line. The home team had made the initial first down of the game. Chip moved closer to the sideline so he could get a better view of the action. Speed followed his lead.

The Eastern quarterback came right back with another pass. This time it was to his wide end on a fly play along the right sideline. The long-legged sprint star outran Aker, got a half step lead on Miller, and caught the ball over his outside shoulder without breaking stride. Miller made a desperate dive for the fleet runner and brought him down on the State thirty-yard line.

"Man alive, fifty yards in two plays," Speed muttered in exasperation, expelling air from his puffed cheeks.

Hansen called a time-out and looked toward the bench. Ralston nodded and two long strides brought him to Chip's side. "In for Ward, Hilton. Speed, for Aker. Miller shifts to Aker's cornerback position. Hurry! Look for another pass right away. Get them organized out there, Hilton. Tell Miller to play the flankerback head to head about five yards back. And tell him to stay with him no matter where he goes. Chip, you double up with Finley on the wide end. Tell Hansen to blitz. Hurry!"

Side by side, Chip and Speed sprinted out onto the field, called to the players they were replacing, and hustled into the huddle. Chip barely had time to complete Ralston's instructions before time was up. He and Speed backtracked to their defensive spots, the same positions they had played together since they had been high school sophomores back at Valley Falls.

Remembering the blitz, Speed moved forward so he could cover the hole over center. Chip edged to his left and eyed the wide end.

Time was up and Eastern burst confidently out of the huddle. And, just as Ralston had warned, the quarterback faded back and got set for another pass. Chip grinned appreciatively as Monty, Maxim, Biggie, Whitty, and Hansen put on the rush. They were through the line and on top of the Eastern running backs before the passer had a chance to get set.

Instead of eating the ball or using a flare to one of his pocket backs, the quarterback attempted the original play. But he had overlooked State's new middle linebacker. Hansen dashed up the opening like a storm whips down tornado alley. His long arms were extended high above his head. He got a piece of the ball, and it wobbled over the center of the line.

As if playing in tandem, Speed raced in, dove forward, and captured the interception just before the ball could reach the ground. It was State's ball, and first down on its own ten-yard line!

Hazzard reported for Whitty, Jacobs for Miller, Anderson for O'Malley, and Soapy for Hansen. In the huddle, Chip called for a draw play with Fireball carrying. "On one!" he said. "Brush-block. Let 'em come through. Let's go."

They broke out of the huddle, and Chip took his position behind Soapy. He glanced toward Hazzard in the wide-end position on the left and then toward Jacobs in the flankerback spot on the right. "Set!" he called. "Hut! Hut!—"

Soapy passed the ball on the first hut, and Chip dropped back into the passing pocket, pumping his arm as if to pass. The Eastern front line rushed and filtered through. At the last moment, however, Chip slipped the ball to Fireball. The big power runner found a hole in the middle of the line and bulled his way up to the State twenty-three-yard line for the first down.

They huddled quickly, and Chip called for a fly pass to Hazzard with Jacobs making the throw off of a reverse to the left. "On three," he said.

The Statesmen came up to the line and Chip called, "Set! Hut! Hut! Hut!"

Fireball drove into the line. Chip faked to him and then handed off to Speed. Anderson pulled out of the line, and Speed followed him to the right. Jacobs timed it just right; he took the ball from Speed and followed Chip and the rest of the reverse blockers to the left where they formed a pocket.

Hazzard was crossing the midfield stripe when Jacobs dug in behind his blockers and fired the ball. The speeding wide end broke into the clear and was wide open when he pulled in the ball on the Eastern thirty-yard line. He crossed the Eastern goal line, standing up, ten yards ahead of the nearest pursuer.

As soon as he crossed the goal line, Hazzard joyously tossed the ball high in the air. A moment later he was surrounded and hoisted to the shoulders of the jubilant Statesmen. Jacobs and Hazzard had combined to complete a spectacular seventy-seven-yard pass, forty-seven in the air and thirty on the ground!

The official recovered the ball, placed it on the two-yard line, and blasted his whistle. "Play ball!" he commanded.

State formed in placekick formation, and, with Speed holding, Chip kicked the point after. The score: State 7, Eastern 0.

Following the touchdown, State played a purely defensive game. On the offense, Chip relied on running plays from the split-T and resorted only to sideline and deep bomb passes from the shotgun formation. The rushing of State's front line throttled the Eastern passer, and the linebackers, with Hansen in on every tackle, smothered the home team's running attack.

Despite the outstanding game they played, the Statesmen were forced to make two goal-line stands to thwart Eastern's desperate attempts to score.

Chip's punting was sensational and kept Eastern pinned down in its own territory throughout most of the second half. When he had the wind at his back, his high, spiraling kicks kept Eastern deep in its end of the field. Against the wind, he got off two beautiful quick kicks from the shotgun formation that caught the Eastern safety players by surprise. Each kick cleared their heads and rolled nearly to the goal line. Each time the ball was downed by State's pass receivers.

It was a bitter, desperately fought game between two evenly matched teams. Jacobs's pass to Hazzard was the only score of the game. State left the field victorious, lucky to escape with an unexpected underdog upset. The final score: State 7, Eastern 0.

Chip congratulated Hansen for his fine defensive play. Chip's hometown pals, honoring Chip's request, joined in recognizing Hansen's accomplishments. Greg Hansen shrugged off their praise and lapsed into his usual shell, but it had little effect on the rest of the players. Yelling, cheering, and laughing gleefully while they showered and dressed, they celebrated the big victory. Then, collecting their personal gear, they hustled out of the locker room and piled into the waiting buses. Minutes later, the buses got underway and headed back toward University.

Just as the coaches knew it would, the singing started before the buses left the Eastern Campus and continued all the way to the Village Restaurant where chicken dinners were waiting, as per Murph Kelly's instructions. On road trips, Murph Kelly, as senior trainer, was responsible for meals and other travel arrangements. And, by the time they had finished eating, the Eastern evening paper had caught up with them. The delivery man was bewildered by the rush of players, and the dozen or so papers he usually left with the restaurant cashier were sold before he had time to make change for the first sale.

Most athletes start reading a newspaper with the sports section before turning to the front of the paper for the national and local news. Soapy led the rush and followed the custom.

"Ahem! Ahem!" the redhead called loudly. "Champs! Fellow teammates! Lend me your ears! Last night this very same paper called Eastern a three-touchdown cinch to win today's game. The reporter even had the audacity to declare that the home club's benchwarmers would be able to get some game experience against us. Well, tonight the paper reads a little different. Listen to the headline: 'State stuns Eastern 7-0.' Ha!

"'The home forces were shocked and stunned by a greatly underrated—' Now that's more like it!

"'. . . By a greatly underrated team that scored early on a seventy-seven-yard pass that caught Eastern by surprise and then played a tight defensive game to win by the score of 7-0.'

"And get this! 'The Statesmen's front four throttled Eastern's famous passing attack, and the visitors' line-backing trio, led by a giant middleman, stopped the locals' running attack cold.

"'Offensively, the visitors scored on their second play of the game. After State's safety back, Speed Morris, intercepted a pass on his own ten-yard line, Fireball Finley found an opening in the Eastern line and carried for a thirteen-yard gain. On the next play, Chip Hilton called a perfect play. It was set up to look like a reverse and ended up with flankerback Jackknife Jacobs throwing a bomb to Flash Hazzard, the visitors' wide end. The pass was good for seventy-seven yards and the only touchdown of the game.'

"Well," Soapy gloated, "Eastern's varsity wasn't so hot, and their benchwarmers must have caught some bad colds. They didn't play a single second! Now for the frosting on the cake. 'Coach Curly Ralston's Statesmen came quietly into town by bus, unheralded and unranked. Then, after ending Eastern's two-year winning streak with a sophisticated offense and a tenacious defense, they left town rated as a national powerhouse.'"

Soapy paused and looked triumphantly around the crowded restaurant. "Well, what do you think about that?"

The cheer that followed shook every table in the place, and Murph Kelly had to stand up and glare at the players before they would quiet down. Then, after a variety of desserts and with their appetites satisfied, the exultation simmered down. The boys tramped back to the buses and were on their way once more. The singing started up again, but, just as the coaches had expected, it gradually died out, and when the drivers dimmed the lights in the buses, most of the players settled back for a snooze.

The postgame letdown had gripped Chip, and he lapsed into a pensive silence, his thoughts ranging from the game to Hansen, the offensive to the defensive lineups, from his job at Grayson's to his university studies and the tough games to come in their schedule.

State had been declared the victor today, but there was a long road ahead. As the season wore on, the lack of adequate depth and the ever-present injury jinx would haunt Ralston and his staff and take their toll. Today, the defense had functioned efficiently because most of the outstanding offensive team players had played both ways. How long could they keep it up? Offensively, the team was all right with the exception of a good pullout man in the right-guard spot. Hansen was the logical choice, but that meant that he, too, would be called upon to play both ways.

If, and it was a big if, Hansen would even consider such a move.

The buses pulled into University just after one o'clock, and Chip was glad when he reached Jeff and could go to bed. He was asleep almost as soon as Soapy turned off the light. Even so, it seemed only an hour or so before Soapy's alarm clock jarred him awake. He glanced at the clock and could scarcely believe his eyes. It was ten o'clock, and he, Fireball, and Soapy were due at Grayson's at eleven.

It was a long day for Chip, but not for Fireball and Soapy. When Chip had occasion to leave the stockroom, he noted that the fans were lined up three deep in front of the fountain. Fireball was taking it in stride, smiling and nodding and working steadily. Soapy was just the opposite. He was in his glory and loving every second of it. With gestures that ignored the half-filled glasses and dishes with which he accentuated the details, the redhead never stopped his description of the game.

Later, at Pete's Place, Chip, Soapy, and Fireball had their first opportunity to read the Sunday papers. The local sportswriters were lavish in their praise of State's new wonder team and freely predicted the conference championship and a bid to the Rose Bowl.

Fireball shrugged off the predictions, but Soapy ate them up. "We win the conference," he chirped happily, "and then it's the big bowl. We'll kill 'em!"

CHAPTER 13

Scrapbook Story

STATE'S BIG WIN over Eastern University, as a good win often does, kindled a feeling of team pride in the players' hearts. For the first time that season, the locker-room atmosphere reflected the spirit of a winning team. Murph Kelly had printed a big sign on the bulletin board. The sign was the first thing Chip saw when he reported for practice Monday afternoon.

CONGRATULATIONS, CHAMPS!
LIGHT UNIFORMS TODAY.

The players were kidding and joking and rehashing the game as they dressed for the workout. Although the comeback effort had taken a lot out of the players who had played both ways, they cheerfully ran out on the field full of energy and determination. But they weren't fooling Ralston. He had coached too long and too well. After the team calisthenics, wind sprints, and some light group work, he wisely dismissed everyone for the day.

As soon as they had showered, dressed, and stowed their gear, Chip, Soapy, and Fireball piled into Fireball's old yellow VW and headed for Grayson's. George Grayson's pride and interest in his employees had built up a tremendous spirit of loyalty. Chip and his coworkers weren't due until seven o'clock, but it was ten minutes to five when they checked in. Chip went directly to the stockroom and began filling department requisitions.

The stockroom intercom buzzed a short time later, and Chip picked up the receiver. Mitzi told him a lady was waiting to see him. "A Mrs. Hansen," she added.

"I'll be right out," Chip said, cradling the receiver.

Mrs. Hansen's visit was so unexpected that he experienced some anxiety. What if something had happened to Mr. Hansen? Chip hurried to the front of the store and found Mrs. Hansen standing beside the cashier's desk. He could see that she was embarrassed, so he tried to put her at ease. "This is a pleasant surprise," he said, smiling.

"More like an imposition," she replied. Then the words tumbled out swiftly as she continued. "I shouldn't have come here at all, but I just had to thank you for your interest in Greg. He has been a changed person since the day you visited with us. He has so few college friends, you know."

"I like Greg, Mrs. Hansen."

"He has quite a few problems to overcome, and he really needs a good friend. I was wondering if you would like to come visit with us again this coming Sunday. We would like to have you come to dinner. Besides, the high school boys keep asking when we're having you back."

"I would like to come."

Mrs. Hansen's face brightened. "Your visits mean so much to Greg. It, well, it gives him standing with the high school boys and takes his mind off of things he shouldn't worry about." She placed a hand over her mouth and shook her head. "I guess I shouldn't have said that. As usual, I talk too much. We'll look for you on Sunday."

"I'll be there."

The practices were demanding and long the rest of the week. Ralston was taking no chances on overconfidence. He continued working with the defensive unit, using Aker, Hansen, and Roberts in the linebacker positions and Ward and Miller in the safety spots.

Offensively, he alternated Chip and Ward at quarterback, Morris and Miller at running backs, and Billy Joe Kerr, a promising sophomore, with Finley at fullback. The right-guard position was wide open, but Riley and Spencer were receiving the most attention.

Chip was worried about Ralston's obvious intention to use Ward and Miller in the safety positions. He liked Miller's speed and tackling ability, but felt the local quarterback was out of position. For the life of him, he couldn't forget the first two passes in the Eastern game. Both had been long and directed toward Ward and Miller. Thinking back to the camp breakup game, he remembered Ward's defensive weakness against Montague and Whittemore, both tall receivers. Offensively, Ward had a strong arm and a fighting spirit, but he was short and lacked running speed.

Chip's pals were also worried and upset. They met each night at Jeff just before bedtime and discussed Ralston's Western game plan. Chip joined them but said nothing about the combinations and lineups. His teammates were not so reticent. Friday night, the discussion was particularly open. Soapy took the lead and frankly said what he thought.

"Ralston isn't going to win the big games with those guys," he said bluntly. "Spencer and Riley aren't fast enough to get out of their own way much less get out in front of Chip. Actually, they're more of a hindrance than a help. Every time Chip calls for a rollout, sprint-out, or a spinout, I shudder. I know exactly what's coming. He's going to get smeared."

"We've got some tough games coming up," Speed added soberly. "Midwestern, Southwestern, A & M—take your pick. They're all tough. And they're all undefeated. Besides, they have half a dozen scouts watching us every time we play. They know *exactly* where we're weak."

"Defensively," Monty said quickly.

"Not if Ralston lets enough of us play both ways," Fireball retorted.

"Well, I'm not worried about Chip," Biggie said quietly, "but I *am* worried about Ward, offensively and defensively, Miller as a safety man, and Riley or Spencer in the running guard job."

"Let's not second-guess the coach," Chip interjected. "I think we should let him do the coaching, and I think we should take each game as it comes. Right now, we've got Western to worry about. Tomorrow!"

"We'll kill 'em!" Soapy growled.

That was the general team attitude when the Statesmen took to the field the next day. And they had lots of company. The State fans were talking proudly about the unexpected Eastern win. All were jubilantly confident and looking forward to an overwhelming victory over Western.

The visitors won the toss and the captain chose to receive. Chip kicked off to the visitors' goal line, and the receiver ran the ball out to the twenty-yard line. Then, following his game plan, Ralston kept his big front four—Montague, Cohen, Maxim, and Whitty—in the game and sent Hansen, Roberts, and Kerr in to back up the line, Aker and Jacobs to guard the corners, and Ward and Miller for the safety positions.

On the first play, Western lined up in a shotgun offense, and the quarterback immediately passed to his towering tight end. Ward and Miller had the big fellow sandwiched, but he went up above them and came down with the ball on the Western forty-nine-yard line.

Another pass and a reverse carried to the State twenty-six-yard line, and Hansen called for a time-out. He looked toward the bench for help. Ralston replaced Jacobs, Roberts, and Kerr with Morris, Finley, and Chip. But it was too late. The Western players were hungry and kept their momentum going. The quarterback hit his wide end on a down-and-out pattern that took the ball to the State five-yard line.

It was first down and goal to go from the five. The quarterback sent his power back into the line, but Hansen and Maxim stopped him cold at the line of scrimmage. Then, faking a pass, the Western field general ran an end-around play. The big tight end picked up a wave of blockers and carried the ball across the goal line for the touchdown. The kick for the extra point was good and Western University led, 7-0.

The State fans were still confident when State lined up to receive. Chip caught the ball on the goal line and made it to the thirty-yard stripe before he was tackled. Ward and Miller replaced Chip and Speed once again. The State offense couldn't move, and Ralston sent Chip back in to punt. He got a high floater away and the Western receiver called for a fair catch on the visitors' thirty-five-yard line.

Once again, Ward and Miller ran in to replace Chip and Speed in the safety positions. And, once again, Western came out of its huddle and lined up in the shotgun formation. Everyone in the stands knew what was coming, and the fans rose en masse and called, "Pass! Pass! Watch for a pass!"

Standing fifteen yards behind the line of scrimmage, and with four receivers spread across the field, the Western quarterback had only his power back to defend him against the State rush. The receivers sprinted upfield on the pass from center, and it was the wide end who broke loose. He outran Ward and Miller, and the quarterback managed to get the ball in the air. It looked as if the quarterback had overthrown his receiver, but it was a high pass and the runner ran under the ball and made a fingertip catch on the State fifteen-yard line. Although he was off balance right after he caught the ball, he kept his feet.

Ward and Miller were right behind the end, but he regained his stride, changed direction, and beat them to the goal line for the touchdown. The try for the extra point was good, and Western now led 14-0.

The mood in the stands had shifted. The State fans were upset and angry. They had read the sports pages and they were aware of State's reserve problem. Further, they were willing to go along with Ralston's efforts to give his new players some game experience. But not to the point that a game could be lost. Not to a team like Western! That was too much!

Some of the fans began to shout advice to Ralston and others added their opinions. Then some of the students began chanting, "We want Hilton! We want Hilton! We want Hilton!" and the chant spread and gained in volume until it was a thundering roar.

Chip was ashamed of himself, but he agreed with the fans. A loss to Western could ruin the whole season. He nudged Speed and walked closer to Ralston. State elected to receive, and when Ralston looked around and nodded, he and Speed raced in to replace Ward and

Miller in the runback spots. The Western kick was low and straight to Speed. Chip led the way and took out the first man he met. The kickoff safety man barely managed to drop Speed on the forty-yard line.

The quarter ended on the play and the teams changed goals. Now the Statesmen were fighting mad, fired up by the support of the fans, and determined to get back in the game. Chip called for the split-T and stayed with it as State marched down the field. With Fireball smashing through the line and Speed turning the corners, the Statesmen scored in nine plays. Chip deftly converted the point after. The score: Western 14, State 7.

Neither team could score in the second period, but Chip's superior punting forced the visitors back and kept them pinned down in their own end of the field. The half ended with Western still leading 14-7.

In the third period, Ralston tried Ward once more, hoping that he and Hazzard could unleash their famed passing attack. But the big Western forwards blitzed Ward repeatedly, and Hazzard was double-teamed. Western's free safety intercepted one of Ward's bullet passes and ran it back for a touchdown. Western lined up in placekick formation and shocked everyone by faking a kick and completing a pass in the end zone for a two-point play. The score: Western 22, State 7.

In the fourth quarter, Chip took Western's kickoff on the goal line and made it back to the State forty-yard line. He immediately passed to Montague for a gain of fifteen yards. Then, with the ball on the Western forty-five-yard line, Speed cut off tackle for twenty-two yards, and it was first down and ten on the Western twenty-three.

Chip faked a pass and used Fireball on the draw. Finley cut through the center of the line, veered to the right, and, picking up two key blocks by Hazzard and

Anderson, crossed the goal line untouched. Chip again kicked the extra point. That made the score Western 22, State 14.

State's defensive team now consisted of Montague, Cohen, Maxim, and Whittemore on the front line; O'Malley, Hansen, and McCarthy in the second line of defense; and Miller, Morris, Finley, and Chip in the secondary. It was a fighting defense. Chip kicked off a high floater to the Western five-yard line, and the receiver was downed on the twenty. The visitors could not gain and were forced to kick. The punt carried only to the midfield stripe, and Chip ran the ball back to Western's forty-yard line.

Ralston sent Riley in for Hansen, Hazzard for Whittemore, Smith for O'Malley, Anderson for McCarthy, and Jacobs for Miller. Using the split-T and hitting inside with Finley, off-tackle with Speed, passing to Monty in the flat, and using sideline passes to Hazzard and Jacobs, Chip led the Statesmen to the Western twenty-five-yard line. The Western captain called for a time-out.

When time was in, Fireball carried through the middle for three yards. Speed slipped off tackle for four yards, and that made it third down and three yards to go with the ball on the Western eighteen. Then disaster struck.

Chip called on Jacobs for a sweep around right end. Just as the flankerback turned the corner, he fumbled the ball! Trailing the play, Chip beat the Western strong safety to the ball and recovered it on the Western twenty-two-yard line. He scrambled to his feet and called for a time-out.

It was fourth down with seven yards to go, and Chip and Cohen trotted to the sideline to confer with Ralston. The coach studied the clock and then turned to Rockwell. "Pass?" he asked.

"We have plenty of time left," Rockwell said thoughtfully. "I think Chip should go for the three points."

"Chip can do it!" Biggie said. "We'll take the ball away from them after the kickoff."

Ralston turned to Chip. "Your decision, Hilton," he said tersely.

"I'll try the placement."

"You'll *make* the placement," Rockwell said calmly.

Back in the huddle, Chip called the play, and the Statesmen lined up on the Western twenty-two-yard line in placekick formation. The fans were really furious and their cheers turned to boos. On the second "hut," Soapy spiraled the ball back into Speed's waiting hands, and Chip booted it straight and true over the goal line and between the uprights for the three-pointer. That made the score Western 22, State 17.

Six minutes were left to play in the game when Western received Chip's kickoff. The receiver made it to the twenty-five-yard line. Then, keeping the ball on the ground and using all the time possible between plays, the Western quarterback tried to run out the clock. But State held the visitors on their own forty-yard line, and the Westerners were forced to punt. The kicker angled the ball out-of-bounds on the State twenty-two-yard line. That stopped the clock with less than two minutes left to play.

The Western coach sent in a secondary defense composed of halfbacks and his regular safety men. Chip countered with State's shotgun offense and took to the air. He had been using short, sideline passes to Hazzard, and now he called the fly and asked Fireball for good protection. Soapy's pass was perfect. Chip retreated clear back to the ten-yard line before the Western rushers reached him. Hazzard had avoided the two defensive players who had been dogging him and Chip let the ball go. It was a perfect peg! Hazzard caught the ball over his outside shoulder on the midfield stripe and made it to the Western thirty-four-yard line before he was hit. His wits solidly in control, he twisted his body and fell out-of-bounds on the tackle to stop the clock.

Chip used Jacobs on a reverse pass to Montague that was good and took the ball to the Western eighteen-yard line. As soon as Monty was down, Chip called for State's last time-out. There were only five seconds left. In the huddle he called for a cross-over end-zone corner pass with Monty and Jacobs screening across in front of Hazzard.

To gain time, Chip attempted a rollout to the right. But his interference collapsed, and he was forced to reverse direction. There, he ran into the weak-side rushers and barely managed to get the ball in the air before he was hit and hurled to the ground. He didn't see Hazzard catch the ball, but he heard the crowd's tremendous roar, and he knew the flashy wide end had caught the ball for the winning touchdown. Hazzard's tally put State in front 23-22, and a minute later Chip's placekick scored the final point of the game. The score: State 24, Western 22.

The fans rushed onto the field, moving through and around the field security as if they were made of paper. The players never had a chance to get off the field, but they loved every minute of it. Once again, Chip and his teammates had come from behind to win a game that was all but lost.

Sunday afternoon, after another one of Mrs. Hansen's wonderful dinners and after spending an hour with the high school athletes, Chip and Greg walked slowly to the corner where they had parted that first Sunday. Strangely pensive, Greg stopped and leaned back against the corner telephone pole. Chip waited patiently for his new friend to say what was on his mind.

"Are you in a hurry?" Greg asked at last.

"No, Greg. Why?"

"Well, I would like to explain some things to you."

Chip realized that Greg was undergoing considerable mental stress and tried to help him. "Take your time," he said.

"Well," Greg began, "strange as it may seem to you, I feel that you're my best friend. I think I should explain a few things that may account for my actions."

"It isn't necessary."

"I want to. I'm sure you've noticed my father's aloofness. First, I want to explain that. My father's study has been off-limits to me as long as I can remember. But, one day, when I was just a freshman in high school, I went into his study to get some writing paper. I pulled out a drawer of his desk and found a scrapbook.

"I opened the book and found a picture of a young man and a young woman. It was a picture of my parents when they were in high school. My father was sitting in a wheelchair, and the story below the picture told all about the injury that had crippled him.

"It was all there, his greatness as a fullback and the wonderful football future ahead of him. Clipping after clipping emphasized his sensational accomplishments as a fullback. He came from a family of fullbacks, and the story stressed the fact that Hansen men felt a good fullback could make a great team. A great fullback, a great team. In those days, I guess, the fullback was the most important player.

"There were other stories, too, ones that weren't so happy. Stories of my father's disappointment and how badly he had wanted to play college and professional ball and be a coach.

"Near the end of the book, I read about his marriage to my mother. That wasn't all. There was another clipping . . . a small article about me. It was . . . well . . . it told about my adoption by Mr. and Mrs. Hansen."

Greg paused for a moment and then plunged on. "The story about the adoption hit me hard. I had never dreamed that Mr. and Mrs. Hansen weren't my parents. I slipped out of the study and, after a while, well, I guess I got used to it. But I never forgot the struggle they had faced in adding me to their burdens and the sacrifices they made in helping me through school. I really don't know how they have made ends meet." Greg's voice broke, and he paused for a few seconds.

"They have been very kind to me and wholly unselfish in giving me the love and opportunities they would have given their own son. I wanted desperately to help some way. They wouldn't let me quit school and get a job, so I made up my mind to be a good football player, a fullback. Not only to get a scholarship, but for Mr. Hansen's—"

"For your father's—" Chip interrupted.

"For my father's sake. I could have gone to several other big schools, but I wanted to play for State and be close to home. I thought that way he might get to see me play and perhaps it would help him forget his affliction and restore some of the love he used to have for football.

"The obsession, or whatever you want to call it, has always been with me. I was determined and I still am determined to play fullback. I had the same trouble in high school that I have here. The coach wanted to use me as a tackle, so I quit and went out for soccer.

"Then, at junior college, I finally made fullback, and I couldn't wait until I could get in the university. You know the rest." Greg stopped, and Chip and he shared the deep silence that means so much to close friends.

Chip was thinking of his own father and the close similarity of Greg's life to his own.

"I know how you feel, Greg," Chip said gently. "My father played football here at State and made all-American. He was killed in an accident when I was a little boy. Like you, I dreamed of following in his footsteps. And my mother has worked very hard for many years to keep our home going and to help me through school."

They stood quietly and without speaking for a long time. Then Chip grasped Greg's hand. "Thanks for trusting me, Greg. I'll never forget your confidence. See you tomorrow at practice."

Chip hurried away. Greg's story had changed all his thinking. Chip was determined to see Greg Hansen get his chance to play fullback if and when an opportunity came along.

CHAPTER 14

Mismatch Contest

CURLY RALSTON was an early riser and led a rigorous life from the first day of training camp to the last game of the season. Every player was aware of the coach's daily routine, but Chip probably knew Ralston's habits better than any of the others. Monday morning, Chip beat Soapy's alarm clock by half an hour and was waiting on the steps of Assembly Hall when Coach Ralston arrived.

"What are you doing here?" Ralston asked.

"I wanted to speak to you about Greg Hansen, Coach."

"What about him, Chip?"

"Coach, he's had his heart set on playing fullback for you ever since he checked in at Camp Sundown. He feels that if he got a little experience at fullback this year, he would have a good chance to take Fireball's place next year."

"I know all about Hansen's fullback aspirations, Chip. We tried him at fullback several times in camp, as you know. But we're convinced that he can't blend in with our plans for next year's offense. Besides, he will be a senior next year. Kerr will be a junior. We have to look to the future. We'll have Kerr for two more years. No, Chip, Kerr is the logical replacement for Finley. He has a lot to learn, but all he really lacks is experience. Hansen is just learning our key defensive position and that in itself is a tremendous accomplishment."

"I'm sorry, Coach."

"Don't be, Chip. You can always talk to me about whatever is on your mind. In fact, right now, I'd like to discuss Miller and Ward. We're leaning toward Miller as a backup player for you and at cornerback on the defense. He's fast, has a good arm, and has shown enough defensively to qualify him for a cornerback job. We have given up on Ward as a quarterback and are going to try him as a backup player for Jacobs.

"So far, we have tried to develop a permanent defensive platoon without success. In fact, the effort to find defensive teams to take care of opponents' kickoffs and plays from scrimmage has resulted in near-defeats in games that should have been easy victories.

"Despite the fact that mental and physical fatigue are major contributors to injuries and the possible loss of games, we've decided to go all out and try to win the conference championship by playing most of you both ways. Years ago, before the platoon system came into existence, a varsity player was expected to play both offense and defense. Substitutes were just that—players who replaced a regular. As you know, we've played many players on both offense and defense in the past. Not all the time, of course, but when we found it necessary. Now you run along and start looking forward to a lot of work offensively and defensively every game from now until the end of the season."

Chip's heart leaped. That was what he had been waiting to hear. Now State could *really* open up. "Yes, sir!" he said. He pivoted and could hardly restrain himself from leaping and shouting in joy. "See you later, Coach!"

Chip had no classes until that afternoon, so he decided to go down to Grayson's and catch up on some stockroom work.

Later that afternoon, the coaches began preparing for the Midwestern game. Always near the top of the conference and always a contender for the championship, the game was to be played on the road. It would be a tough one. A defeat might well ruin State's hopes for the conference title. By Friday afternoon, when State arrived for the crucial test, Ralston was satisfied that his team was ready.

The usual pregame road routine was followed that night and Saturday morning, and when the Statesmen ran out on the field that afternoon, they were well rested. It was a perfect day for football. The sun was bright and warm, there wasn't a cloud in the sky, and there was no wind to bother the kickers and passers. The huge Midwestern Stadium was filled to capacity, and the bright colors in the stands and smartly dressed band and cheerleaders added to the excitement that can be generated only at a college football game.

The home team won the toss and elected to receive. Chip booted the ball back to the goal line, and the ball carrier carried the ball out to the thirty-yard line. Ralston had started a kicking team that had his big four on the line: O'Malley, Hansen, and McCarthy in the linebacking positions; Miller and Finley on the corners; and Speed and Chip in the safety positions.

On the first play, the Midwestern quarterback sent his wide end and his flankerback into Miller's cornerback territory. Skip pursued the wide end, and Speed picked up the flankerback. Then the tight end on the other side of the line got away from Finley. He cut behind Hansen, and, in the clear, dashed down the middle. Fearing a bomb, Chip chased him clear to the State twenty-five-yard line.

Hansen had called for the normal defense against a running play, and the front four did not rush. That gave the passer time to get set, but none of his key receivers was open, so he threw a safety pass to his right running back. The area was wide open, and the runner was away and had carried the ball to the State thirty-five-yard line before Chip left the end and brought the ball carrier down.

State held at that point, but the pass had placed the Statesmen in a hole. Although the home team failed to score, it kept the Statesmen's backs to its goal line for the rest of the quarter. After they changed goals, Chip went to work with his short passing and running game. He hit Hazzard with safety sideline passes. He connected with Montague and Miller with passes over the middle and in the flat, and he varied his pocket passes with rollouts and jumpers. To keep the defense honest, he used Speed and Fireball through the line on power plays and draws. The result was a steady march down the field. When the Statesmen reached the Midwestern thirty-yard line, the home team captain called for a time-out.

When time was in, Chip used Ward for the first time on a reverse around right end. Chip faked a jump pass, pivoted, and handed off to Whip, and the chunky little flankerback carried the ball to the fifteen-yard line. Then Chip went to Finley, and the rugged power back bulled his way to the Midwestern four-yard line in just three plays. Then, combining with Ward on a fake reverse, Chip hit Hazzard in the corner of the end zone for the touchdown. With Speed holding and Soapy making his usual accurate pass, Chip booted the ball between the uprights for the extra point. The score: State 7, Midwestern 0.

Neither team could gain during the rest of the quarter, and it ended with State in possession of the ball on its own forty-yard line. The score at the half still remained State 7, Midwestern 0.

State received to start the second half. Chip mixed his safety passing game with short running plays by Fireball and Speed. The Statesmen ground out the yardage needed to carry to the home team's twenty-yard line before they were stopped. On fourth down, Chip booted a three-pointer field goal, and State led 10-0.

Midwestern was desperate now, and the quarterback went for the bomb on the first play from scrimmage. But Chip anticipated the pass and knocked the ball down on the State forty-five-yard line. The rest of the quarter went scoreless. In the final period, an exchange of punts resulted in Midwestern being pinned down on its own ten-yard line. The frantic quarterback attempted a bomb to his wide end, but again Chip went to Miller's aid. Timing his move perfectly, Chip dashed in front of the speeding wide end and intercepted the ball. He reversed in a wide circle and began to pick up blockers. First it was Miller, then Speed, then Ward, and then Finley.

Each took out a man, and Chip sped down the sideline with only the quarterback between him and the score. Then he saw Biggie and changed direction in time for the big tackle to upend the quarterback with the key block that enabled Chip to score the touchdown. He kicked the point after, running up the score to State 17, Midwestern 0.

Midwestern received and immediately went to the air. They managed to reach their own forty-five-yard line but were forced to punt. The Statesmen took over on their own seven-yard line. Chip now resorted strictly to running plays to beat the clock, and the game ended with the ball in State's possession on the Midwestern thirty-yard line. The final score brought the Statesmen a respectable win: State University 17, Midwestern University 0.

That night, after the usual steak dinner, Ralston gave the Statesmen a midnight curfew and advised them that the entire squad had been invited by the women's basketball and volleyball teams to a concert at Midwestern University. A show of hands left only Chip, Biggie, Hansen, and Hazzard not caring to go.

Instead, the four opted for a movie. After the film, they grabbed a snack at a fast food restaurant and then returned to the hotel. Chip was in his room and in bed at 11:30. Soapy checked in at five minutes to twelve bubbling over with a recital of his conquests. He had a list of fourteen girls he had met at the concert and, of course, all had been smitten by his charm and football fame.

"I promised to E-mail each of them," he said.

"What about Mitzi?"

"Now why did you have to bring her up?" Soapy complained. "You've spoiled my whole evening."

"Oh, sure! You better get some sleep. We've got to leave for the airport at seven o'clock, and that means Kelly will be prowling the halls at six. Good night."

It seemed as if he had been asleep only five or ten minutes when their wake-up call pierced the sweet stillness of the darkened room. Chip could hear the phones ringing in the rooms on either side of theirs, and a few seconds later Murph Kelly began knocking on doors, calling for the players to "Hit the deck."

"He must still think he's in the Navy or something," Soapy quipped as he brushed his teeth with one hand

and stuffed his sweat pants into his duffel bag with the other.

"Smith! Hilton! Be in the lobby in twenty minutes. No fooling around now, Smith!"

"Smith?" Soapy complained, his toothbrush still jammed in the corner of his mouth. "Why am *I* always the one he picks on? Why, I'm as innocent as a lamb, I am, I am!"

Everyone was in the lobby on time. The sleepy players loaded their gear into the underbelly of the chartered bus and then piled on for the fifteen-minute ride to the private airport where the State University chartered jets awaited them, ready to speed down the runway.

On the planes, after a light breakfast, some of the players read the papers, a few studied, but most slept. When the planes landed at the private runway adjacent to University Airport later that morning, the terminal was swarming with enthusiastic fans carrying banners, posters, and even painted bed sheets welcoming home their State University victors.

Carrying their personal belongings, Chip, Soapy, Speed, Biggie, and Fireball managed to get away from the fanfare and boarded the team bus as quickly as possible. Back at Assembly Hall, the friends transferred their gear to Fireball's VW and Speed's Mustang, squeezed in, and headed back for the dorm and some peace and quiet. Chip and Soapy attended church services, grabbed a quick lunch at Furr's restaurant, and then met up with Fireball at Grayson's. The three friends worked through the afternoon and evening and then skipped the usual get-together at Pete's Place, opting for a quiet evening back at Jefferson Hall.

Soapy and Fireball joined the dorm gang in the kitchen, popping popcorn and microwaving pizzas, but Chip went directly to his room. It had been a long weekend, and he felt completely bushed. Now he realized what Coach Ralston meant by mental and physical fatigue. Despite the great win over Midwestern, there was a long road ahead of the Statesmen. Even more worrisome, every time they went on the field from now on, the injury jinx would hover over every block and every tackle and every kick and every pass.

The campus and the town were buzzing with football talk the next day. The students and many of the town fans were talking about "their" team and the conference title. Many were already making plans to accompany the Statesmen to Pasadena to see a Rose Bowl game for the first time in their lives.

But Curly Ralston and his coaching staff weren't about to court overconfidence and risk a letdown in team morale and condition. Northern State had sustained several losses, but it was the underdog team that most frequently caught fire and upset a highly ranked team. The coaches worked the Statesmen hard all week.

Friday afternoon, the Statesmen took to buses for the trip to Albion for the Northern State game. They checked into the hotel, enjoyed their team meal, sat through the usual pregame skull session, and then went to a movie en masse. They were in bed at 11:00 and up at 9:30 the next morning. They ate their pregame meal at 10:30, dressed at 12:00, went through their warm-up routine at 1:15, and were back on the field and ready for the game at 1:50.

Chip won the toss and elected to receive. The game got under way exactly at two o'clock. He and Speed were standing just outside each of the goal posts when the Northern State fullback kicked off. The ball carried to the ten-yard line, and Chip waved for Speed to make the catch. Then he cut out in front of Speed to lead the way. Up ahead, the wedge was forming perfectly with Hansen in the point position. Chip headed for the center of the funnel. The first opponent to break through the wedge was a big, heavy lineman, and Chip's shoulder block knocked him off balance and to the ground.

Speed dashed through the hole, broke to the right sideline, and nearly—yes, nearly—got away. The kicker brought the speedster down just over the midfield stripe. It was first and ten on the Northern State forty-five-yard line.

Chip sent Fireball through the middle and the blockbuster picked up seven yards. Speed went off tackle for six, and the Statesmen had a first down on the opponents' thirty-two-yard line. Chip dropped back, faked to Hazzard, and then hit Monty, who was cutting behind the linebacker. The big end carried to the eighteen-yard line for another first down.

Then Chip faked another pass and sent Fireball through the middle on the draw. Fireball went all the way. Touchdown! Chip's point after was good, and State led 7-0 after a mere four plays from scrimmage.

The Northern State captain chose to receive, and as Chip trotted back upfield for the kickoff, he felt that the game was a mismatch. He wasn't counting the home team out, but if the Northerners' offense was no better than their defense, they had no business being on the same field with the Statesmen.

He kicked off to the goal line, and the receiver barely made it to the fifteen-yard line before he was buried under a mass of State tacklers. Now Chip was sure. Three plays later, he was positive. Northern State's offense proved to be as bad if not worse than its defense. The opponents couldn't gain an inch, and Speed took the fullback's punt and ran it back to the home team's thirty-seven-yard line before he was brought down. From there, State scored in five plays, and Chip again kicked the extra point to make the score 14-0.

Ralston began substituting freely and continued to run his reserves in and out as he gave most of his regulars a rest. He used Kerr most of the game at fullback with Spencer and Riley alternating at the right-guard position. The game was a tremendous letdown for the regulars, but the reserves enjoyed every minute of it, romping to an easy victory. The final score: State 42, Northern State 0.

The locker-room horseplay was missing after the game, and Chip was glad when he and his teammates got away from the Northern State campus. They ate dinner at a local hotel and were on their way back to University at seven o'clock.

Chip almost always sat with Soapy on a bus or plane trip, and he was particularly glad that was the case on this trip. His heart went out to Hansen because, in his own mind, Greg was a better fullback prospect than Kerr. He wished Ralston had given Greg a chance to show what he could do. His thoughts went flying ahead to the games coming up. Only four games remained to be played: Cathedral, Wesleyan, Southwestern, and A & M. And they were all tough. Cathedral, defeated only by A & M, was capable of beating any team on a given day. Wesleyan had lost only to Southwestern. Wesleyan boasted a high-scoring offense, but Southwestern had pulled all the stops to win a torrid, free-scoring contest by a score of 47-42.

Then would come the vital game with Southwestern. If the Statesmen got by that one, the conference championship might be decided in the final game against A & M. Then he remembered his advice to his teammates: Take the games as they come and win them one at a time. Well, the first was Cathedral.

CHAPTER 15

Bitter Memories

THE SCOUTING REPORT on Cathedral was thorough, complete, and, to say the least, ominous. The Irishmen were big, tough, and fast. Offensively, they liked to stay on the ground and grind out their yardage from Chip's favorite formation, the split-T. Defensively, their front line was massive and speedy, and the secondary defenders were quick and played a tight man-to-man pass defense.

Chip and his teammates had followed the progress of all the conference teams, and they had read the newspaper reports of Cathedral's only loss. According to the articles and TV reports, the Cathedral–A & M game had been a knock-down-drag-out affair. The two teams had battled scoreless for fifty-nine minutes. Then, with less than a minute to play, Cathedral had attempted to pass from the A & M thirty-yard line. Kip Kerwin, A & M's all-American running back and free-safety star, had intercepted the ball on the Aggie ten-yard line and made a ninety-yard run to score the winning touchdown.

With the newspaper clippings and the scouting notes to warn them, the State University players buckled down and worked that week as they had never worked before. By Saturday morning they were prepared for a do-or-die effort against their toughest opponent to date. The sky was clear, and it was just cold enough to make it a good day for a hard game of football. The players dressed, went through their pregame warm-up routine, and returned to the locker room for Ralston's final review of the game plan. Then they returned to the field and huddled in front of the State bench.

The stadium was packed with fans also expecting a tough fight, and they were eager to support their home team. Red and white decorated nearly two-thirds of the stands, but the visiting section was nearly filled with Cathedral's orange and white. With the cheers of the fans and the State University Fight Song ringing in their ears, Chip and Hansen ran out to the middle of the field to meet with the officials and the Cathedral captains. There was no wind, and the choice of goals was of little importance. The Cathedral captain won the toss and surprised Chip and Greg when he chose to kick. Chip said he would defend the north goal. Two minutes later, the Statesmen were aligned in receiving formation in front of the north goal.

A burly kicker immediately booted the ball into the State end zone, and Chip realized the reason for the Cathedral captain's choice. Cathedral had an expert kickoff artist. In the huddle behind the twenty-yard line, Chip called for a power thrust with Fireball carrying. But when he reached the line, the Cathedral linebackers began stunting, leaping into and back out of the line again. Chip then used his audible signals and switched to a jump pass over the line to Monty.

The play worked perfectly. Soapy passed the ball just as the middle linebacker sprang forward and into the line, and Chip leaped up in the air and hit Monty in the hole behind the middleman. Monty carried the ball to the thirty-two-yard line before the strong safety brought him down.

Following Ralston's offensive game plan, Chip shifted Jacobs to the right flankerback position and Hazzard to the wide-end position on the left side of the field. He then called for a reverse pass. Faking to Fireball driving into the line, Chip handed off to Jacobs, and the flankerback picked up his moving-pocket blockers and cut to the left. Stopping in the pocket, Jacobs threw a bomb to Hazzard, who was sprinting on the fly play far down the field.

The Cathedral right cornerback couldn't stay with Hazzard, and the free safety shifted over to help out. Changing direction, Flash cut directly toward and then past the free safety to break free into the open. Jacobs released the bomb, and Hazzard caught the ball on the Cathedral thirty-yard line. Completely unscathed, he crossed the goal line. The Statesmen had scored in just the first three minutes of the game! Chip kicked the extra point, and State led 7-0. What a start to this ball game!

Cathedral received and Chip booted the ball into the end zone. Now the visitors opened up with their split-T formation and tried to run through State's line. But their big forwards couldn't move State's front four, and Hansen met the ball carrier and dropped him on the line of scrimmage. They tried two more line thrusts, and then their kicking team came in and punted to Chip on the forty-yard line. He made it back to midfield before he was stopped. That placed State in position to use everything in the book in their effort to score again.

Calling for a pitchout to Speed, Chip rolled out to the right. But the opponents' left linebacker moved out to stop Speed. Chip kept the ball and picked up six yards before the middle linebacker and the cornerback downed him. It was second and four for the first down on the Cathedral forty-four-yard line, and Chip had yet to test the middle of Cathedral's line. He called on Fireball for one of his power line drives. The big fullback drove straight ahead behind Maxim and Riley, carrying for five yards and the first down.

Chip used another rollout and hit Speed with the pitchout this time. The fleet sprinter turned the corner and carried the ball to the Cathedral twenty-six-yard line for *another* first down. The visitors held them there, but Chip kicked a successful field goal to end the quarter with State in the lead 10-0.

Neither team scored in the second quarter, and State left the field at the half still leading by ten points. When halftime ended, State lined up for the kickoff. Chip booted the ball all the way to the Cathedral goal line. The runback receivers took a look at the first wave of State tacklers and let the ball bound into the end zone and out-of-bounds for the touchback.

Starting on the twenty-yard line, the visitors managed to grind out their initial first down of the game. On the next play and for the first time, the quarterback attempted a pass. It was intended for the wide end. Fireball was playing him head to head, and in attempting to catch the ball, both went out-of-bounds and landed in a tangle of arms and legs in the middle of the gear in front of the Cathedral bench.

The visitors' end scrambled to his feet, but Finley did not get up. He remained on the ground in a sitting position, grasping his right leg with both hands. Doc Terring and Murph Kelly rushed across the field, and the referee called a time-out. Chip was right behind Murph and saw Fireball point to the first-aid box.

"I landed smack on top of that thing," Fireball said. "My leg feels numb and I can't move it."

"Don't try," Doc Terring said quickly. "Murph, bring a stretcher."

Kelly called two of his assistants, and they rushed across the field with a stretcher. With the help of two of the student managers, they carried Fireball off the field. The fans and students rose to their feet and stood quietly until the stretcher bearers had carried Fireball the length of the field. Then they began to applaud and continued until the little group disappeared through the players' exit.

Aker replaced Fireball at right cornerback and the game continued. The Cathedral quarterback tried his fullback on a draw play up the middle, but Greg Hansen dumped him at the line of scrimmage for no gain. The quarterback attempted another pass to his wide end, but Chip knocked it out-of-bounds. It was fourth down when the Cathedral kicking team ran onto the field. Chip and Speed waited for the ball back on the State thirty-five-yard line. It was a high kick, and Chip was forced to signal for a fair catch. Ralston sent Soapy in for Hansen, Anderson for O'Malley, Riley for McCarthy, Jacobs for Miller, Kerr for Aker, and Hazzard for Whittemore.

Chip now went to the air. He pitched a flare to Speed Morris that was good for three yards and attempted a sideline pass to Hazzard. The Cathedral cornerback and free-safety player were double-teaming Hazzard, and all three went up for the ball. Hazzard caught it, but when the three players came down, he was on the bottom, just out-of-bounds. The umpire ruled the pass incomplete. Hazzard got slowly to his feet, clutching his shoulder. Ralston immediately sent Whitty in to replace him.

Chip tried a jump pass to Monty over the line, but the tight end was hit the instant he caught the ball. It was close to a first down, but the referee motioned to the head linesman to bring in the chain for the measurement. When the chain was stretched out from the thirty-five-yard line, it showed the ball was short of the first down by a foot.

Chip kicked the ball to the Cathedral twenty-five-yard line, and the receiver made it back to the thirty-yard line before Monty and Biggie decked him. Ralston sent in the defensive team, and the Cathedral quarterback went back to his ground game, managing to make two first downs in a row. The quarter ended at that point and the teams exchanged goals.

The fourth quarter was a repetition of the third. Both defensive teams were superb. When State was on the offense, Chip took no chances; he protected the ten-point lead by keeping to ground plays and depending on his kicking and his defensive teammates to hold Cathedral in check.

With the clock running out, the Cathedral quarterback tried several desperation passes, but State's secondary functioned perfectly. With less than two minutes left to play in the game, Chip intercepted a long pass and ran it back across the midfield stripe. Checking the clock, he kept the ball on the pass from Soapy and carried it into the line twice in succession. Time ran out as State came out of its huddle. The final score remained State 10, Cathedral 0.

Chip and his teammates hurried off the field. They were anxious to learn the extent of the injuries to Fireball and Flash. Ralston was right behind them. When they crowded into the locker room, Fireball was

lying on the rubbing table while Kelly applied com-
presses to the injured leg. Doc Terring was completing
a pressure pack on Hazzard's shoulder.

"Nothing is broken, Coach," the physician said reas-
suringly. "Hazzard has a badly bruised shoulder, and
Finley will be limping around with a bad muscle knot
in his thigh for a week or so. I will need a picture of
Hazzard's shoulder before I can give you a full report
on him."

"You'll call me."

"Sure will. I'm taking both of them to the medical
center in a few minutes."

"I'll be home all evening."

The coach shook hands with each of the injured
players. "Sorry," he said sympathetically. "I'll be in to
see you first thing in the morning."

At the door, he turned and waited until the players
quieted. "Congratulations for a fine victory. It was a
complete team effort. By the way, no prac—"

The players' cheer drowned out the rest of his sentence. Ralston smiled and closed the door behind him.

Chip and Soapy decided to walk to work. For the
first time that season, the redhead was down in spirits.
From working the fountain together, Soapy and
Fireball had become close pals, and Soapy was worried
about his buddy. Chip went directly to the stockroom
and remained there until it was time to go home. There
were orders to inventory and shelve. Then, skipping
their nightly snack at Pete's Place, Chip and Soapy
jogged home to Jeff and went straight to bed.

Sunday afternoon, after church services, Chip and
Soapy had an hour to spare and made a visit to the
Hansen neighborhood playground. The field was
buzzing with activity. Chip located Greg running signals with the high school players. One of the younger
kids sighted him and led the others in a mad dash in

his direction. When they flocked around him, Chip introduced Soapy. The redhead took over the way only Soapy could. The kids loved him!

Chip wandered toward the high school players. Greg saw him and dropped out of the signal practice. "I was hoping you would come," Greg said. "Do you think Coach Ralston will give me a chance at fullback against Wesleyan?"

"I don't know, Greg."

"Will you ask him for me?"

"Sure, but I don't know whether it will do any good."

"I sure hope so. Thanks, Chip. Want to join in the practice?"

"No, we just stopped by to say hello before going to work. Did you get any lumps yesterday?"

Greg smiled and nodded. "Sure did. I've been trying to run them out. They were tough. It's a good thing we got out in front in a hurry."

"It sure was. See you Tuesday at practice."

"Hope you have some good news."

"Me too. So long now."

He rejoined the group surrounding Soapy and managed to get the redhead away from the youngsters. "I'll be back," Soapy assured them. "You guys try that play I was telling you about."

Chip and Soapy worked Sunday afternoon and evening and all day Monday. After lunch on Monday, Mrs. Hansen came into Grayson's and asked for Chip. He joined her at the cashier's booth and invited her to sit down at one of the tables in the food court. "How about a soda or some ice cream?" he asked.

"No, thanks, Chip. I just stopped by because I wanted to explain Mr. Hansen's sports attitude."

"I know quite a bit about his background, Mrs. Hansen. When we played in Eastern, I looked up his name in the library and read about his football accident."

Mrs. Hansen sighed. "Then you know he was a great player."

"Yes, I do."

"It was his whole life," Mrs. Hansen said softly. "He had scholarship opportunities all over the country. The injury shattered everything for him, his dreams of college and professional football, and his ambition to be a coach. In fact, he grew to hate the game. I tried to help him with his problem, but it was impossible.

"John always felt the fullback was the *man* of the team, the man of strength. And then, suddenly, he was unable to walk, much less play. I tried to interest him in college study, but he had no interest in it. I went to business college, and after I graduated, we were married.

"John's mother had been dead for several years, but when his father died, I felt we should move away from Eastern and make a fresh start. I thought it might help. But when we moved, John withdrew even more within himself. Nothing seemed to remove the bitter memories. Then, fortunately, Greg came along and we moved again. This time we settled in University. I was lucky enough to secure a good position at the college.

"John has never lost his aversion to football. His only pleasure the first few years of our marriage was Greg. He loved Greg deeply, and he would hold him in his arms and tell him stories by the hour. Then Greg began to grow up big and strong, and filled with the desire to play football, and all the bitterness came flooding back.

"He made me promise never to tell Greg about his football accident because it might make the boy unhappy. John felt that Greg's desire to play football should come from within and because of a burning love for the game, not for any other reason, you see?

"John has never complained, then or now, about his handicap. He simply retreats within himself."

Mrs. Hansen paused. "I thought that if you knew about my husband, you would understand why Greg is so confused. I . . . well . . . I don't want to burden you with our family problems, but I do want you to know how much I appreciate your interest in Greg. You have been a great help to him."

"I want to help him, Mrs. Hansen," Chip said understandingly, "and I will."

After Mrs. Hansen left, Chip returned to the stockroom. Everything was coming into focus. Greg didn't have the slightest concept of the feelings behind his father's attitude toward football!

Freak Trick Plays

CHIP STOPPED by Coach Ralston's office Tuesday afternoon. When he tapped on the main door, Coach Rockwell's secretary, Mary Ann, beckoned him to come in. "Hi, Chip. I'm just getting things ready for the upcoming basketball season—it'll be here before you know it! What's up?"

He told the friendly secretary he wanted to see Coach Ralston. She immediately called the coach and nodded to Chip. "You can go right in."

The door to Ralston's office was open. The coach smiled and waved Chip to a chair. "Don't tell me it's Hansen again," he said with a sigh.

Chip nodded ruefully. "Yes, sir, it is."

"Knowing him, it figures. Now what?"

"He thought . . . well, he hoped . . . you might give him a chance at fullback while Fireball is laid up."

"He thought wrong. We went over this once before, Chip, and the answer is still no. With three key games coming up, it would be foolish to risk an injury to that boy just because he wants to play fullback. Further, Wesleyan has two powerful runners, and I'm worried about our linebackers. Forgetting Hansen, you must remember that O'Malley and McCarthy are both converted tackles and are playing in the linebacking positions for the first time. If we were to lose Hansen, we would be in a precarious position. With Finley out, I am hard-pressed to find anyone who can handle the cornerback job.

"Now I would like to ask *you* a question. Just why are you so interested in Hansen playing fullback?"

Chip was stuck. He hadn't expected the question and didn't know how to answer it without violating a personal confidence. Then he realized that he could speak with authority about Greg's knowledge of the running-back plays. "I've seen him running our plays on Sundays with some of the high school players, Coach. He knows them perfectly."

Chip realized that Ralston had been studying him closely. "You've brought Hansen a long way since training camp, Hilton. I hope you can keep him coming."

"We're becoming pretty good friends, sir."

"I realize that, and I know just why it came about. I take it Hansen no longer feels he's a better fullback than Finley. Is that true?"

Chip shook his head doubtfully. "No, Coach, I don't believe Greg has come that far. But he *is* looking forward to next year, and he would like to have a chance to show you what he can do."

"I'm sorry our plans do not permit us to do that right now, Chip. Rockwell, Sullivan, and I discuss every player and his potential abilities time after time. Hansen and his fullback aspirations have been taken into full consideration, but the coaching staff's consensus remains the same. We feel it would be a waste of time. In addition to Kerr, Bull Andrews, our freshman fullback, possesses many of Finley's qualities. I wouldn't be surprised if he became our number-one power back next year.

"Now," Ralston concluded, "I have a staff meeting. I appreciate your interest and thinking. You are a fine captain and I wish for your sake that I could go along with Hansen, but I can't. See you this afternoon at practice."

Chip realized that Ralston had been extremely considerate.

"Thanks, Coach," he said. "I appreciate your patience with me."

He thanked Mary Ann, walked slowly down the ramp and out through the main doors, and headed across the parking lot to the Field House. Chip now faced the task of telling Greg that the decision was the same. Knowing Greg as he did, there was no way to figure what the temperamental linebacker's reaction might be.

There was no opportunity to talk to Greg during practice and that gave Chip another day's reprieve to prepare for his reaction. Wednesday, the coaching staff concentrated on the Wesleyan scouting notes and the game plan and again there was no opportunity to talk privately.

Thursday, it was different. Ralston called an early quarterback session, and Greg was included in the list of players. This time, Greg was waiting for Chip in front of the Field House. "Did you have a chance to talk to Coach Ralston?"

Chip nodded. "Yes, I did. I'm sorry, Greg, but Coach's answer was the same as before. He's worried about Wesleyan's offense and feels that you're too important as a linebacker, especially since you are quarterbacking the defense. I'm sorry."

"So am I," Greg said grimly. "I don't know what I'm going to do. I need some time to think."

"We'll have plenty to think about after he gets through with us this afternoon. I suggest you forget everything until Saturday and see what happens in the game. I told Coach Ralston you knew the plays, and you never can tell what will happen in a tough game. Just suppose Kerr got hurt and Roberts too! It *could* happen."

Greg nodded, and they continued on to the lecture room. The Wesleyan offense and the names of the players were written on one of the whiteboards and the formations and key plays they used on the other. Ralston and Rockwell pointed out Wesleyan's strengths and weaknesses and went over every phase of the game plan. Then they dismissed the players for practice.

The workout on the field was comparatively light but extremely important. The players knew there would be no heavy work for the rest of the week. Coach Ralston was fearful of injuries.

Saturday morning, when the Statesmen reported to dress for the Wesleyan game, they were in high spirits. Coach Ralston and his staff had worked more intensely on the Wesleyan game plan than any other so far during the season, and the players took this as a good sign. Further, Ralston's game plans always seemed to work out.

The stadium was packed with fans when Greg and Chip went out to the center of the field for the coin toss. Chip called heads and won. "We will receive," he said.

The Wesleyan captains chose to defend the north goal. After shaking hands with them, Chip and Hansen trotted back, joined in the team handclasp, and ran out on the field with the receiving team players.

Standing beside Speed near the goal, Chip evaluated the offensive team. The line was composed of Monty, Cohen, Anderson, Soapy, Riley, Maxim, and Whittemore. Speed and Jacobs would be in their regular positions with Kerr at fullback.

Chip took the ball on the kickoff and raced to the twenty-six-yard line before he was downed. Using Speed off tackle, reverses by Jacobs, and short passes to Monty and Whitty, he led the Statesmen to the Wesleyan forty-yard line before the visitors' defense held. Chip then angled a punt out-of-bounds on the Wesleyan thirteen-yard line. The visitors' dreaded offense went into action. The game was shaping up to be all that the scouting report had indicated it would be, and more!

The attack featured reverses, passes off of reverses, laterals, passes off of laterals, and a number of freakish trick plays obviously planned to thwart State's defensive linemen. And they worked! The passer had an extremely strong arm, and he was quick. The fullback was a smaller edition of Fireball. He ran like a streak of lightning. Once he found an opening in the line, he was through it and gone with the speed of a track star. Further, he was hard to bring down.

Wesleyan marched up the field and scored the first touchdown in eleven plays to lead, 7-0.

State received, but the running attack was throttled and Chip was forced to punt. He got away a high floater that enabled Monty and Whitty to get down under the ball. The runback receiver let the ball go. It rolled to the five-yard line where Whitty downed it.

Wesleyan's offense managed to reach the forty-yard line, but here the State defense held and the visitors were put in a punting situation. But they faked the punt and the fullback broke away and carried to the State forty-five-yard line. Then, on the first play following the first down, the Wesleyan quarterback fumbled! Cohen recovered the ball on the midfield stripe.

Now State's offense began to click and reached the visitors' twenty-two-yard line, where it stalled. On fourth down, Chip kicked a successful three-pointer as the quarter ended. The score: Wesleyan 7, State 3.

Chip kicked off to the Wesleyan goal line. The runback receiver cut toward the sideline and handed the ball to the fullback. The power runner was on his way! It was a planned and well-practiced play, and two blockers headed directly for Chip. He was the only Statesman between the speeding runner and a touchdown, but he never had a chance to make the tackle. The blockers had him in the middle and cut him down at midfield. The fullback outran Speed and Miller to score. The conversion was good. The score: Wesleyan 14, State 3.

The two teams fought up and down the field, but neither could score, and the half ended with Wesleyan still out in front 14-3.

Wesleyan received to start the second half, but State held on at the visitors' thirty-yard line. Wesleyan's punter came in and got away a high kick. Waiting on the State thirty-yard line, Speed tricked the oncoming tacklers. Faking to catch the ball, he waited until the last possible moment and then dashed past the tacklers and caught the ball on the thirty-five-yard line. Sprinting recklessly, he raced past several tacklers and made it to the Wesleyan thirty-yard line before he was brought down.

So far, Speed and Chip were the only State backs who could gain on the ground. Kerr was fast, but he lacked Fireball's power and experience. That enabled the Wesleyan front-line players and the linebackers to key in on Speed and Chip. Chip called for a screen pass in the huddle and sent Whittemore far to the right in the wide-end position. When he came up to the line behind Soapy, he looked first at Whitty and then at Monty. When Soapy passed the ball to him, he backed up, faking a throw to Monty. The blitz was on, and the Wesleyan rushers filtered through the line. Chip hit Speed, who was waiting behind the State forwards, and then the sprinter was on his way! Using the linemen to screen him away from the Wesleyan tacklers, Speed streaked past the secondary and across the goal line to score State's first touchdown of the game. Chip made the conversion to make the score: Wesleyan 14, State 10.

Wesleyan received and advanced the ball to the thirty-five-yard line as the quarter ended.

There were fifteen minutes left in the game, and the Statesmen were trailing by four points. State's front four were blitzing on every play, leaving the linebackers to make the tackles. The move stopped the Wesleyan passing attack, and the visitors were forced to punt once more.

Chip caught the ball on State's thirty-five-yard line and was dropped hard on his own forty-two. He limited his offense to the running of Speed and short passes to Monty and Whitty. The attack functioned, and State made three first downs in a row. With the ball on the Wesleyan twenty-four-yard line, the visitors took a time-out. State's attack stalled, and Chip kicked another field goal. Wesleyan led by one point, 14-13.

Chip kicked the ball low to the Wesleyan receivers. It landed on the visitors' thirty-five-yard line and bounded back to the twenty, where the runback player was downed just as he picked up the ball. Again, State's front four began blitzing on every play, leaving the linebackers to make the tackles. Wesleyan was forced to punt from its own thirty-yard line.

Chip took the ball on the State thirty-five and was again hit hard before he had taken two steps. The tackle knocked the wind out of him, but he got up and made it into the huddle. There, Biggie took one look at him and called for a time-out. When time was in, Chip had his breath back and called the play. "Jacobs on the reverse. Lots of blocks. On two!"

On the second "hut," Soapy passed the ball to him. Chip handed off to Jacobs, who was cutting around right end. The blockers did a good job, and Jacobs made it to the Wesleyan forty-eight before he was tackled. A slant off tackle by Speed picked up two yards. Now Chip tried Kerr. Billy Joe gave it all he had, but the big Wesleyan forwards smashed him to the ground for no gain. Now it was third and eight, and Chip's pass to Whittemore was good for five yards. That put the ball on Wesleyan's forty-one, on the fourth down and with three yards to go. Chip called for a time-out.

The clock showed three minutes left to play when Chip reached the sideline. Ralston and Rockwell were in a huddle when Chip joined them. "Too long for a placekick," Rockwell said.

"There's not enough time left if we fail to complete a pass," Ralston said thoughtfully. "If only we had Finley—"

"I can kick it over the goal line," Chip said. "If we do that and hold them there, we might block the punt or force a fumble. I'm sure they won't pass. Not with time running out."

"It's a bad gamble," Ralston concluded, "but we have no alternative. Punt it!"

Chip hustled back to the huddle and called the punt.

"Oh, no," Speed cried. "It's only three yards. Let me carry it."

"They've got a stacked line waiting for you," Biggie growled. "Do as Chip says. We'll hold 'em."

"That's it!" Chip said. "On three. Let's go!"

Standing twelve yards back behind the line of scrimmage, Chip waited for Soapy's pass. On the third "hut," Soapy spiraled the ball to the perfect spot, and Chip took his two steps and kicked the ball. He put all his leg strength into the kick and sent the ball over the goal line. It landed in front of the goal and bounded out-of-bounds. He had put more than his foot into that kick; he had added anger and frustration.

Ralston sent in his defensive team while the officials were bringing the ball out to the twenty-yard line. Chip took advantage of the time to call the players into the huddle. He wasn't going to wait on Greg to call the defensive play now, whether the defensive captain liked it or not.

"It's now or never," he said sharply. "We've got to have that ball, and we've got to take a chance." He turned to Hansen. "Call a rush, Greg. The rest of you open up that line for Hansen. Greg, you try to get through or over it and tackle that quarterback. Right now! This down! Remember, it's a stacked line and the rush is on. I'll take care of the pass possibility."

The teams formed, and when the Wesleyan center passed the ball to the quarterback, State's line charged. Hansen was back three yards from the line of scrimmage, but he went over the center—and over Maxim and Cohen as well—and landed on the quarterback's back just as the signal caller turned to complete a handoff. And the quarterback fumbled!

The ball went bounding back behind the running backs. Greg followed it, scrambling along the ground. He just managed to beat the running backs and thrust himself forward at the last second to scoop the ball back under his chest. Then the Wesleyan ball carriers and the quarterback and half a dozen other opponents piled on top of him, with every player in the tangled mass trying to steal the ball away from Hansen.

The officials fought their way into the mass of players and began pulling them off and away from Hansen. He was at the bottom of the heap, but he had his arms and legs and body curled around the ball. The referee leaped up and pointed dramatically toward the Wesleyan goal, and Chip called for a time-out.

It was State's ball, first and ten, on the Wesleyan nine-yard line.

Ralston sent in his offensive players, and this time Ward replaced Jacobs.

When time was in, the roar from the stands drowned out the signals, and Chip had to ask the referee to call for quiet. But it was a futile gesture. The fans were past any reason, unable to do anything except yell and shout and scream in an attempt to release the emotional pressure that filled every fiber of their beings.

The play was for Speed off tackle, and the flashy ball carrier darted into the line and slithered through an opening for a gain of four yards. Now it was second down and goal to go with the ball on the visitors' five-yard line and twenty-five seconds left to play in the game. And State had no time-outs left to call.

Chip used the audible in the huddle, grabbed Monty by the arm and shook it, and led his teammates up to the line of scrimmage. He knew the blitz was on, but there was nothing he could do about it. Time ran out as Soapy passed the ball back. Scurrying back in the pocket, he saw the Wesleyan rushers swarm through the left side of the line and over Kerr, blocking Monty from his view. He turned to his left and saw Ward streaking into the end zone and looking over his left shoulder. That meant a squareout to Ward's left, and Chip drilled the ball toward the little flankerback with all his strength.

The ball hit Ward on the chest and almost bounded away. But Whip reacted with lightning speed and, clutching desperately as he fell, managed to pull the ball in and gain control of it before he fell to his knees for the touchdown and the points that won the game 19-14.

With the stands in pandemonium, Chip kicked for the extra point. The final score: State University 20, Wesleyan University 14.

CHAPTER 17

Forgotten Tomorrow

THE WESLEYAN game left Chip mentally and physically exhausted. The contest had drained his mind of its sharpness, and every muscle in his body ached. It was times such as these that he wondered whether or not football was worth all the practicing, all the playing, and all the knocks an athlete had to take.

Coach Ralston had removed the Saturday night training curfew, but that meant nothing to Chip. He had no plans for the evening. All he cared about was getting home to Jeff and sleeping in late on Sunday morning.

Not so for Soapy! Grayson's was jammed all evening, and the redhead entertained his fans by extravagantly describing his part in the victory. He was still going strong when closing time rolled around. Soapy hurried back to the stockroom and changed out of his striped polo shirt and white slacks, his Grayson's fountain uniform. He replaced them with a pair of dress slacks, a button-down shirt, and a sports coat.

"Come on, Chip," he said. "Let's get going. We're invited to Pete's for a celebration. Steaks and the works, all on Pete."

"Count me out," Chip said wearily. "I'm going home. You go ahead. But don't you dare wake me up in the morning!"

"I'll probably just be getting home when you wake up," Soapy said cheerfully. "Well, I gotta get back to my public. Oh! Nearly forgot. Did you hear about Coach Ralston's father? Some of the guys told me about it a little while ago—"

"Told you what?"

"About Ralston's father. He lives somewhere out in California, and he was watching the game on television. He had a stroke. I think he's OK, but Coach left right after the game. Coach Rockwell is in charge of the team till Ralston gets back. I gotta run. See you later."

Soapy rushed away. Chip locked up the stockroom and started for Jeff. It was a beautiful fall night. The stars were cut crystal in an inky blue sky, and the smell of turning leaves filled the air. Chip walked slowly up Main Street and across the campus shortcut to the dorm, thoroughly enjoying the solitude. On the way, he thought about Coach Ralston and his father and offered a prayer for a full recovery. When he reached Jeff, several students were sitting in white wicker chairs on the porch and talking to Fireball and Flash Hazzard. Chip paused and asked Fireball and Hazzard how they were coming along.

"Not good!" Fireball said gruffly. "Doc Terring says neither one of us can play in the Southwestern game. How do you like that?"

"I don't."

"I'm OK right now," Fireball contended. "My leg is stiff, sure, but I could run that out if he would let me."

"Me too," Flash added. "You could hit that shoulder cup with an ax and I wouldn't feel it."

"Perhaps Terring is kidding," someone suggested.

"Him?" Fireball said. "He never kidded anyone in his life."

"Could I talk to you a second, Chip?" Flash asked. "Privately?"

"Of course. Come on up to my room." Chip led the way up the stairs, turned on the light, and motioned toward one of the easy chairs. "Sit down. What's on your mind?"

"It's Greg. Greg Hansen. He's going to quit the team."

"You're kidding!"

"No, I'm not. He told me to turn all of his stuff in to Murph Kelly on Monday. He said he was through. He means it, Chip."

"He must be out of his mind. Why, it's the worst thing he could do. He'll never forgive himself if he does that! He played a marvelous game today. He's the most important defensive player on the squad."

"I know. That's why I thought you should know."

"Where can I find him?"

"I don't know. He said he was going out of town for the weekend."

"I'll find him. Have you told anyone else about this?"

"Not a soul."

"Give me your word that you won't. Not even to Ward or Riley, OK? One more thing: Don't say anything to Kelly about Greg turning in his uniform."

"Don't worry about that. Greg is my friend."

Hazzard left, and Chip dropped down on his bed to consider his next move. What next? First Ralston's father and now Greg. *What do I do?* One thing was for sure, he had to act quickly about Greg. If the newspapers ever got ahold of it, the story would be plastered on the sports pages of every paper in the country. And, if Coach Ralston heard that Hansen had quit the team, Greg would never put on a State uniform again. *That* he knew for sure.

"Lord, it rains whenever, but right now, it's *pouring*. Help me to know what to do," Chip prayed earnestly. "I want so much for everything to work out, but only You know how that will go. Please help me not to be discouraged . . . I need to trust You," he concluded. "Lead me in the direction I should go, Lord, be it Greg's friends or even his parents. In Jesus' name. Amen."

Chip sighed and opened his eyes. He knew just how stubborn and bullheaded Greg could be. What was the greatest influence in Greg's life? He loved his mother, but . . . then Chip had it! The person Greg cared most about was his father.

Mr. Hansen was the key. Chip decided he would see him first thing in the morning. "No!" he said aloud. "I'll see him now. Tonight!"

The Hansen home was engulfed in quiet darkness when Chip opened the picket gate. He stood there for a moment, tempted to turn back. Then he thought of the seriousness of the situation and continued up the steps to the porch. He knocked on the door. He waited a short time and then knocked again. A light flashed on in the living room, and then Mrs. Hansen called, "Who's there?"

"It's Chip Hilton, Mrs. Hansen. Is Greg home?"

"No, he isn't, Chip. Is anything wrong?"

"No, Mrs. Hansen, but I would like to talk to you and Mr. Hansen."

"Well, we were already in bed, Chip—"

"It's quite important to Greg, Mrs. Hansen."

There was a short silence, and then Mrs. Hansen said she would call Mr. Hansen. Chip waited, and a short time later Mrs. Hansen opened the door and invited him into the house. Mr. Hansen was sitting in his wheelchair near the door to his room.

"Have a chair, Chip," Mrs. Hansen said, indicating a chair beside the window.

Chip sat down and then plunged in. "I'm awfully sorry that I had to wake you up," he said apologetically, "but Flash Hazzard told me Greg was going to be out of town for the weekend."

"That's right. He's visiting my sister. I can give you her telephone number." Mrs. Hansen went to get a pencil and paper, and Chip waited, uncomfortable under the hard, steady, unyielding gaze of Mr. Hansen.

Mrs. Hansen returned and handed Chip a slip of paper. "Now," she said, "what did you want to talk to us about?"

Mr. Hansen's face remained impassive as he waited patiently for Chip to continue. Chip decided then and there that he would pull no punches.

"First, Mr. Hansen," Chip began, "Greg knows all about your football accident, and he knows you were a great fullback. He has been upset because you have never taken an interest in his progress as a player.

"I don't know whether you know it, but Greg is the most important player on State's defensive team. Besides that, he's the defensive team quarterback."

Chip paused, but when Mr. Hansen said nothing, he continued. "The team needs your help right now, Mr. Hansen. Greg is thinking about, well, about quitting the team—"

"Quitting!" Mr. Hansen echoed impulsively.

"Yes, sir," Chip replied. "Greg wants to quit because he hasn't been given a chance to play fullback. You see, Mr. Hansen, Greg knows all about the Hansen family fullback tradition, and he has been so set on playing fullback because of that tradition that he has caused a lot of trouble for Coach Ralston and some of the players, chiefly Fireball Finley. Fireball is an all-American, but Greg has been so determined to help you regain your interest in football that he has been trying desperately to prove he is a better fullback than Finley."

Mrs. Hansen stirred restlessly. Then she leaned forward and interrupted Chip. "Mr. Hansen didn't know any of this, Chip. If he had known how Greg felt, I am sure he would have been behind him in every respect."

"That's right," Mr. Hansen said. "I never encouraged Greg to play football. I didn't know until recently how far he had come in the game. I always felt that a boy's desire to play any game, especially football, had to come from within, not because of the influence of his parents. I'm glad to know Greg has been so successful, and I'm proud of the fact that he is important to the team. But I am most proud because he did it all on his own.

"I would have been proud of Greg even if he had been only a water boy. A boy doesn't have to play on the first team or even on the reserves. He can be a scrub and still be important to the team. And he doesn't have to play any particular position to be important.

"Once I was obsessed with playing fullback because my father had played in that position and his father before him. I thought it was the only important position on a team. I was wrong. And Greg's wrong if he thinks that way too. There is no *I* in team, and there are eleven positions on a team. All are vital to the success of the team. The big objective is to play together, to be a part of the whole thing.

"Young athletes should remember that football is only a game. Players are heroes today and forgotten tomorrow. I ought to know. Football is only a small part of a man's life. Only a few make football a successful career. Professional football is also just a game. It gives a player prestige and a good start financially, but there is more to life by far than playing football."

Mr. Hansen paused and smiled. "I've talked more about sports tonight than I have for years. Now that the spell is broken, I guess Greg and I will have a little more in common. Now, you said I could help Greg and the team. How?"

"Well, if you could repeat to Greg what you have just said to me, it would help. And, if you could convince him that playing *any* position that helps the team is important, I am sure he would forget about playing fullback and maybe fill in as guard on the offensive team. Our offense would improve fifty percent if Greg would take over the right-guard position.

"Right now, though, the important thing is to make sure Greg reports for practice Monday afternoon."

"He'll be there," Mr. Hansen said firmly.

Chip had never expected a break such as this. He rose to his feet and shook Mr. Hansen's hand. "I've been hoping for this a long time," he said earnestly.

"Me too," Mr. Hansen said cryptically.

Mrs. Hansen opened the door for him and Chip said good night. Hurrying away, he suddenly remembered that he had been dead tired an hour earlier. It was surprising how quickly a fellow's spirits soared and his fatigue disappeared when he was helping a friend.

Teams do not reach the next to the last game of a season undefeated unless they have something big going for them. Southwestern had an unblemished record and a complete offensive and defensive unit. State was also undefeated. They boasted an offensive team that could move the ball, but the Statesmen were forced to depend upon many of the offensive team players in order to present a satisfactory defense.

Through most of the season, State had two all-American players in the lineups of both platoons. Now the Statesmen had only one. Injuries had continued to plague the team. Finley and Hazzard were still sidelined, Anderson was out with a badly sprained ankle, and some of the veterans were suffering from sprains and bruises.

On Monday, almost every player on the squad had been shocked when Greg Hansen promptly volunteered for an opportunity to fill in at right guard on the offensive team. Rockwell had then shifted Riley to the left-guard position, which enabled the offensive line to function with some authority.

A crowd of more than fifty thousand spectators were in the Southwestern University football stadium when the teams lined up for the kickoff that Saturday afternoon. State had won the toss, and Chip had chosen to receive. The Southwestern kicker booted the ball down to the goal line, and Speed brought every person in the stadium to his feet with an electrifying one-hundred-yard kickoff return! Chip blocked the first tackler down the field. Speed flung off another on State's fifteen-yard line, spun away from still another on the twenty-yard line, and raced down the sideline to score the first touchdown of the game. Chip successfully booted the point after to give State a 7-0 lead after a mere fifteen seconds of play!

Southwestern received and staged a grind-it-out offense that marched sixty-five yards downfield to score, with the final play being a beautiful thirty-yard pass to the flankerback in the end zone. The conversion was good, and the score was tied at 7 all. There was no scoring in the second quarter, and the half ended with the teams still tied.

The Southwesterners went ahead when they marched the opening kickoff of the second half back sixty-seven yards to score their second touchdown. That gave Southwestern a seven-point lead, 14-7.

They increased their lead when they recovered a fumble by Kerr on the State thirty-five-yard line and needed only two plays to go ahead 21-7 on a swing pass that was good for thirty yards and the touchdown.

State received and Chip's first two passes to his big ends carried them to the Southwestern thirty-two-yard line. Southwestern's defense held. Chip kicked a forty-yard placekick that brought the score closer together: Southwestern 21, State 10.

After an exchange of several kicks in the fourth period, State scored when Chip intercepted a pass on the Southwestern forty-yard line and sprinted down the side of the field for the touchdown. He kicked the extra point to cut the score to a four-point Southwestern lead, 21-17.

With five minutes left to play, Southwestern tried to run out the clock, but its attack stalled on its own thirty-six-yard line. The visitors' kicking team came in, and Hansen and Cohen teamed up to block the kick and recover the ball on the Southwestern twenty.

Chip shifted Whittemore to the left side of the field in the wide-end position and Jacobs to the right flankerback spot. The play was a double reverse with the ball going from Chip to Jacobs to Speed. Southwestern was looking for the reverse pass, and Speed picked up his interference and scored around the right end untouched. That put State in the lead 23-21. Chip kicked the extra point, and the game ended with the score State 24, Southwestern 21.

Except for Speed's kickoff runback for the touchdown, it had been a dull, uninteresting game. Not that it mattered to the Statesmen. They had won the game, and that was all they cared about.

The score of the A & M-Western game was flashed on the scoreboard just as the game ended. A & M had defeated Western by a score of 34-19. State and A & M, both undefeated, would meet for the conference championship the following Saturday in the Aggies' stadium.

The Statesmen returned to University Sunday morning by plane. When Soapy fell asleep, Chip found an empty seat next to Greg. "How come you knew the guard plays so well?" he asked curiously.

"Because I've been practicing them with the kids ever since you told me about going to the library in Eastern."

CHAPTER 18

Championship Game

CURLY RALSTON was pacing back and forth between the two rows of lockers that edged the locker room under the Aggie stadium. His footsteps were drowned out by the scraping of the mud cleats on the floor and a murmur here and there as players talked to Murph Kelly or one of his assistants.

Chip glanced at the wall clock. It was not yet one o'clock. That left over an hour in which to finish dressing, move out onto the field for the pregame warm-up, return to the locker room for Ralston's talk, and then charge back out onto the field for the introductions, the coin tossing, and the start of the game.

Ralston stopped his pacing at the end of the room and waited for the players to quiet down. "Ready, Murph?" he asked.

"All set and never better, Coach," the trainer said quickly.

"Good! Let's go."

Chip picked up a ball and led the way out of the visiting locker room and along the players' alley that led to the field. Before he reached the exit he could hear the rain and the wind and the crowd noise that meant some of the sixty thousand fans who would watch the game had already arrived.

Chip trotted out of the mouth of the alley and into the driving rain. The sky was gray and unforgiving, and the stadium lights illuminated the field. A cold rain was steadily beating directly into his face, driven from the east by the relentless wind. Then, from the stands behind him, a cheer went up from the bravest of the ten thousand fans who had traveled more than five hundred miles to root for their Statesmen.

Chip led his teammates into a big loop and trotted to the middle of the circle for the team calisthenics. First they were running in place, then doing forward falls with three push-ups, and finally adding a leap-up-and-let's-do-it-all-over-again move. His teammates joined him in the count. After five minutes of that, Chip called it off. Soapy, Fireball, Speed, Whip Ward, and Skip Miller followed him to the side of the field for punting practice. Soapy covered the ball, and Fireball and Chip alternated kicks while the three receivers caught the ball and sprinted back. It was tough going. The turf was wet and slippery, and the ball was slick and threatened to slither out of their hands.

In the center of the field, the offensive and defensive linemen were matched up face-to-face, taking turns punching away at their shoulder pads. Nearby, the ends and linebackers were engaged in short sprints and pass patterns.

Fireball, finally cleared to play, punted several times and decided to get into the shoulder-pad workout. Chip and Skip Miller then took turns passing to Hazzard, Montague, Whittemore, Jacobs, Aker, Ward,

Morris, and Kerr. Twenty minutes later, Murph Kelly blasted his whistle. They trotted back to the locker room.

The clock showed only fifteen minutes to go when Ralston began to talk. He was quietly confident, and his voice was calm and precise. "We've come a long way to get here," he said, a slight smile crossing his lips, "and I don't mind telling you that there were times and days when I didn't think we would make it." He paused and glanced around the room, nodding his head grimly. "But you did it! And here we are in the Aggies' stadium with a chance to take it all. We might be only a couple of hours or so away from an invitation to the Rose Bowl."

He turned toward Sullivan and Stewart. "Turn the board around, Jim, Chet."

The coaches lifted the whiteboard and turned it toward the players. The offensive and defensive teams were listed. Ralston said nothing while the players studied the lineups.

OFFENSIVE TEAM			DEFENSIVE TEAM		
86	Montague	Tight End	88	Whittemore	Left End
79	Cohen	Left Tackle	79	Cohen	Left Tackle
51	Riley	Left Guard	70	Maxim	Right Tackle
50	Smith	Center	86	Montague	Right End
65	Hansen	Right Guard	62	O'Malley	L Linebacker
70	Maxim	Right Tackle	64	Hansen	M Linebacker
83	Hazzard	Wide End	72	McCarthy	R Linebacker
12	Hilton	Quarterback	19	Miller	L Cornerback
33	Morris	Running back	42	Finley	R Cornerback
37	Jacobs	Flankerback	33	Morris	Strong Safety
42	Finley	Fullback	12	Hilton	Free Safety

"Our scouting reports have given you a complete outline of the Aggies' formations and defensive alignments. You know all about their abilities, and every player in this room is as familiar with our game plan as are the coaches. However, Coach Riley and his Aggies undoubtedly have a surprise or two planned for us. No matter. I feel we have the best team—"

A knock on the door interrupted him. "Game time, Coach."

"Coming right out," Ralston called. He turned back to the players and continued. "We have the best team and we're going to win. Remember now, we line up just inside the players' exit and wait until the names are called. As your name is called, you run out between the goal posts and to our side of the field, where you line up facing the Aggies bench. Let's go!"

The players leaped to their feet with a cheer and again followed Chip out the door and along the alley to the mouth of the exit. There, he stopped just out of the rain. The wind was from the east, driving the rain toward the west goal.

His teammates crowded eagerly forward, anxious to get the preliminaries over with so they could get at the Aggies. With the terrible weather, Chip had expected to see empty stands, but both sides and the far end of the oval were now crowded with fans. Many came with umbrellas, others with brightly colored ponchos and raincoats, and some even wore large green garbage bags as protection from the elements.

Coach Ralston joined Chip and motioned toward the field. "Defend the east goal if you win the toss. If they win it and elect to defend the east goal, you might as well kick."

"Yes, sir," Chip agreed.

A student assistant was standing close to the wall, just out of the rain. Now he waved an arm toward the broadcasting booth, and the announcer immediately began the introductions. "Ladies and gentlemen, the

State offensive team! Led by number 12, William 'Chip' Hilton, quarterback."

Before he made a stride, a cheer from the State fans greeted him. Then, as he ran between the goal posts and headed for the State bench, the cheer became a roar above which he could just hear the announcer introducing his teammates one by one.

"Number 42, Fireball Finley, fullback; number 33, Speed Morris, running back; number 37, Jackknife Jacobs, flankerback; number 50, Soapy Smith, center," and so on until he had completed the starting offensive team. Then he began again:

"The defensive unit! Number 64, Greg Hansen, middle linebacker and defensive captain; number 88, Philip Whittemore, left end; number 79, Biggie Cohen, left tackle; number 70, Joe Maxim, right tackle; number 86, Chris Montague, right end," and so on until he had completed the starting defensive team. Then he continued through the alternate offensive and defensive players.

Before the announcer could begin his introduction of the Aggies, a tremendous cheer descended from the stands. The announcer tried and kept at it, but the crowd's roar, the wind, and the driving rain made it impossible to hear the names and positions, much less the numbers. The roar continued and kept right on going when the officials, wearing striped plastic coats, walked out to the center of the field and beckoned toward each bench. Two Aggies players ran out from the other side of the field, and Chip and Greg trotted out to complete the group.

The referee introduced the captains to the officials and to one another and then gave Chip the choice. "Heads or tails, Hilton?"

"Heads," Chip said promptly.

The referee tossed the coin in the air, and it went spinning up above the heads of the players and landed on the wet turf between them. All four players moved forward to see the exposed side of the coin. The spread-winged eagle faced up, and the Aggies captain made his call immediately. "We'll defend the east goal," he said sharply.

"We'll kick," Chip said.

"OK," the referee said. "Let's have a good game and may the best team win." He turned away to demonstrate the results of the toss to the stands, and Chip and Greg shook hands with the Aggie captains and raced back to the State bench to join Coach Ralston and the kickoff team in the center of the circle of players.

Ralston thrust out his hand, and the gang piled their hands on top of his for a moment and then broke out of the circle and formed on the State thirty-five-yard line. The wind was blowing the rain sharply into his face as Chip placed the kicking tee carefully on the forty-yard line and waited for the ball.

The referee had the ball wrapped in a towel and kept it until the A & M captain indicated that his team was ready. Then the official tossed the ball to Chip, and he placed it on the kicking tee and backed up seven yards. The referee blew his whistle, and Chip raised his arm above his head and started forward. He took three short strides, picked up his teammates on the thirty-five-yard line, and, gathering momentum all the while, drove his kicking shoe accurately and with all his strength into the ball. It was a low kick and directly into the wind, but it carried to the Aggies' twenty-yard line.

The A & M receivers were waiting on the ten-yard line, and Kip Kerwin, A & M's all-American halfback, took the ball on the run. He tried to cut to his right, slipped, and went down on his own twenty-five. After the huddle, Stu Hayden, the Aggies quarterback, sent his power back, Rip King, through the middle. But Hansen and Maxim decked him at the line of scrimmage.

Next, Hayden tried a sweep around his right end, but Whittemore, Cohen, and Hansen gang-tackled him on the Aggies' twenty-seven-yard line. A sideline pass to the wide end was overthrown, and it was fourth and seven on the A & M twenty-eight-yard line. A & M's punting team ran out on the field and into the Aggies' huddle. Ralston made only one substitution, Miller for Jacobs.

In the State defensive huddle, Hansen called for a seven-man blitz. But when the Aggies center put the ball in play, Whittemore and McCarthy were the only Statesmen who could break through. The ball carriers blocked them out, and the kicker had plenty of time to get his kick away. It was a beauty. The wind caught the ball and carried it clear down to the State twenty-five-yard line.

Chip and Speed backtracked as the first wave of tacklers came down the field. Speed was under the ball, but he was afraid he might fumble and lifted his arm and signaled for a safety catch. He was surrounded by tacklers, but he held the ball and downed it on the State twenty-six-yard line.

Ralston sent Jacobs in for Miller, Riley for O'Malley, and Soapy for McCarthy. In the huddle, Chip called on Hazzard for a down-and-out sideline pass. It worked like a charm. Hazzard outran the Aggies cornerback and made it to the A & M forty-five-yard line before he was forced out-of-bounds by the free safety.

First and ten now, and Chip faked to Fireball and sent Speed on a tackle slant that picked up three yards. It was second and seven on the A & M forty-two-yard line. Chip faked again to Finley and rolled out to the right behind Hansen. Hazzard was double-teamed, and there wasn't a free receiver in sight, so Chip followed the tall guard and carried the ball down to the A & M nineteen-yard line.

Now it was first and ten, and Chip sent Fireball through the line. Fireball smashed and slipped through to the Aggies thirteen, but there was a penalty on the play. Maxim was charged with holding the defensive left end, and the fifteen-yard penalty brought the ball back to the A & M thirty-four-yard line. It was still first down, but with twenty-five yards to go.

Chip tried a pass to Whitty that was right on target, but the ball was slippery, and the big end couldn't hold on to it. A draw play with Fireball carrying picked up four yards, and now it was third and twenty-one yards to go for the first down. Chip tried Hazzard on a fly play, but the speedster was surrounded, and Chip turned to Jacobs instead, who was cutting along the left sideline. The strong safety picked Jackknife up just as Chip released the pass and managed to knock the ball out-of-bounds.

It was fourth down and long yardage, and Coach Riley loaded his secondary with halfbacks. Chip tried another pass with Jacobs throwing off of a reverse, but one of the Aggie backs knocked the ball down in the end zone.

The officials brought the ball out to the A & M twenty-yard line, and Ralston pulled Chip out for a rest, sending in his defensive team with Jacobs at the left cornerback position and Miller teaming up with Morris in Chip's free-safety position.

When time was in, the Aggies came out of the huddle in their regular I-formation. Chip was standing at the end of the bench concentrating on State's defense, and he sensed the play that was coming. Jacobs was playing Kerwin head-to-head about ten yards behind the line of scrimmage. Finley was playing the Aggies wide end the same way, and Miller was drifting to his left to back up Fireball.

"No!" Chip yelled. "Miller! Cover the flankerback!"

He was too late. Kerwin was away on a fly. McCarthy heard Chip and made a dive for the all-American, but Kerwin was too quick. He slipped past Biff and his race with Jacobs was on. Miller heard Chip a second too late. When he turned, Kerwin had a single-stride lead on Jacobs, and Chip's groan barely preceded the Aggies' fans' roar of exultation.

Now Miller was cutting back toward the goal line, but he was ten yards away when the flankerback crossed the midfield stripe and caught the ball. Jacobs had managed to hold Kerwin to a one-step lead, and when the flankerback caught the ball, Jacobs tried for the tackle. He got a hand on one of Kerwin's heels, but the runner pulled away. The contact had slowed Kerwin down, but it didn't stop him.

Miller managed to reach and tackle Kerwin at State's five-yard line, but the all-American's momentum carried him across the goal line for the touchdown. A & M's kicking team came in, and the boot for the extra point was good. The score: A & M 7, State 0.

The teams battled through a scoreless second quarter, and when the half ended, A & M was still in the lead. During the intermission, the wind died down and the rain slackened.

State received at the start of the second half and advanced to the forty-five-yard line on Fireball's smashes through the line. But A & M stiffened and held, and Chip was forced to punt. The A & M pass defense was perfect. Chip couldn't risk an interception and limited himself to sideline and short, sure buttonhook passes through the third quarter. On third-down plays, he used bomb or long sideline passes. In return, State's defensive unit stopped the Aggies' attack cold, and the game developed into a kicking duel between Chip and the A & M kicker. Finley's running and Chip's superior punting slowly forced the Aggies back, but the quarter ended with A & M still leading 7-0.

The teams changed goals at the start of the fourth quarter, and now the Aggies resorted to delaying tactics, trying to hold their lead while attempting to run out the clock by using every possible second in the huddle. They were relying on ground plays to advance the ball. But State's front four and powerful linebackers held and forced the Aggies to punt. Speed was in the deep receiving position, and the Aggies punter got a high floater away that enabled his first wave of tacklers to get upfield almost as soon as the ball. Chip took out the first man, but others surrounded Speed and he called for a fair catch. The ball came tumbling down into Speed's hands, but—he fumbled the ball!

One of the Aggies fell on it, and the home fans went wild. A & M had the ball just past midfield, in State territory, and ripped off two first downs in a row. Then the Statesmen's defense stiffened, and the Aggies were held to three yards in two plays, and it was third and seven on State's thirty-six.

Back in his free-safety position, Chip was trying to analyze Stu Hayden's thinking. The colorful quarterback had played safe for twelve straight minutes. Would he gamble now? Would he be overconfident, anxious to put the game on ice, and risk a pass?

"Yes," Chip breathed to himself. "Hayden will do just that! He will try an end-zone pass to his favorite receiver, all-American flankerback Kip Kerwin!"

CHAPTER 19

Storybook Finish

A & M CAME OUT of its huddle, and Chip readied himself for a duel with Kip Kerwin. It happened just as if he had written the script. When the center snapped the ball back to Hayden, he scurried back in the pocket and concentrated on his wide end. The Aggies tight end headed straight for Fireball, and the wide end cut to the center of the field with Miller in hot pursuit. Speed backtracked to cover both of the racing receivers. That left Kerwin all alone, and he cut past Hansen and headed for the corner of the end zone.

At the last second and just beating the rush by Monty, Biggie, Maxim, and Whitty, Hayden put the ball in the air. It was aimed for the right corner of the end zone, and Kerwin got there in plenty of time. But the ball never made it! Chip, anticipating this play of a lifetime, timed his move just right, cut in front of the all-American, and picked the ball out of the air and out of Kerwin's hands. Interception! And a beauty!

Running as he had never run before, Chip evaded tackler after tackler. He zigzagged from one side of the field to the other, changing pace and direction with reckless abandon and speed, like a rabbit running for its life. Only Hayden remained between him and daylight. He changed direction again and swerved toward the center of the field just as a tall, red-clad figure flashed past him and upended Hayden with a crashing shoestring block.

Now Chip ran to daylight and the touchdown. Seconds later he was surrounded by his teammates, lifted in the air, and roughed up despite his protests that the game wasn't over and that the touchdown meant nothing unless they scored the extra point.

On the way to the huddle, he debated the next move. Should he go for the conversion or for a run or a pass and the two-pointer? A pass or a running play were good for two points and probably a win. But both were risky. On the other hand, he had never missed a placekick. A tie would mean sharing the title with A & M. Even so, State would still win the coveted Rose Bowl bid. The Aggies had played in the big game the previous year, and a conference ruling prohibited back-to-back appearances.

So, to the disappointment of the State fans, the Statesmen came out of the huddle and lined up in placekick formation. With Speed holding, Chip booted the ball straight and true through the uprights. The score: A & M 7, State 7.

Now the A & M fans were on their feet chanting, "We want a touchdown! We want a touchdown!" drowning out the State fans' "Go! Go! Go!" cheer. As Chip walked into the kickoff huddle, he glanced at the clock. There were less than two minutes left to play. . . .

Ward came tearing into the huddle, replacing Miller, and Chip called the onside kick. "I'll kick to the left," he said, "just past the forty-yard line and ten yards in from the sideline. Biggie and Riley, block. A good block by both of you is a *must!* Ward, Soapy, you fellows bracket the ball and one of you *must* recover it. The rest of you head straight down the field as if for a long kick. They are expecting an onside kick, so the execution must be perfect."

"You kick it, we'll get it!" Biggie growled grimly.

As his teammates took their positions along the thirty-five-yard line, Chip noted that A & M was ready for the onside kick. The receiving team was loaded with halfbacks. Maloney and Breslow, the Aggies' runback specialists, were standing on the goal line, and there *was* a gap right where Chip hoped to kick the ball.

The referee's whistle sounded. Chip lifted an arm and started slowly forward. His kick scarcely cleared the front-line receivers before it hit the ground and careened crazily around on the Aggies' thirty-five-yard line. Chip followed through on the kick and grunted in satisfaction. He had placed the ball perfectly!

Burns, the Aggies tight end, his arms extended and hands clutching hungrily, dove for the ball and tried to claw it toward him. But Biggie crashed into him, and the ball spurted away just as Riley took the closest halfback down with a savage diving block. Soapy took one quick look behind Ward and threw a cross-body block on a player speeding back past the restraining line and—yes! Ward fell on the ball! He barely had time to curl around it before he was buried under an avalanche of Aggies trying to wrestle the ball away from him.

The referee and the umpire were blasting their whistles and pulling the A & M players off of Ward. Then, suddenly and dramatically, the referee straightened up and thrust his arm toward the A & M goal line. It was State's ball, first and ten on the Aggies' thirty-three.

Chip ran toward the referee, leaping up and down with joy, and called for a time-out. The referee nodded, blew his whistle, and pointed toward the State goal to indicate the team to be charged with the time-out. When Chip turned, Fireball was holding Ward high above his head and shaking him as if he were a baby. Others joined in, giving the little quarterback "the treatment" as they carried him back to the huddle.

Chip quieted, refocused his teammates, and called for a pass to Hazzard on a down-and-out fly play. Soapy spiraled the ball back on the third "hut," and Chip fell back in the pocket between Fireball and Speed. The Aggie forwards put on the rush, but Chip had time to get the ball away. Hazzard was still double-teamed, but again Chip tried a high pass, shooting for the end-zone corner. The ball flew out-of-bounds and stopped the clock. It was second down with twenty seconds left to play. Chip verified the time left in the game with the field judge and checked the number of remaining State time-outs with the referee. Then he headed for the huddle. There was time for one more play, perhaps two, if he could stop the clock on the first one. He decided to try another end-zone pass, calling it for Ward this time, on the third count.

Soapy whipped the ball back, and Chip retreated toward the pocket. But he never made it! The Aggies middle linebacker timed his rush, hurdled Soapy, and hit Chip just as he took the ball, smashing him down on the thirty-five-yard line for a loss of two yards. Chip struggled to his feet and called for a time-out. Then he looked at the clock. There were five seconds left and only one more time-out. He hurried toward the sideline.

Coach Ralston was out in front of the bench, talking before Chip reached his side. "It's a long kick," he said.

"Why not try Hazzard or Ward on a goal-post pass?"

Chip shook his head. "If you don't mind, Coach, I would like to use Hansen for a placekick."

"Hansen!" Ralston cried. "Hansen!" he repeated. "Why, I never saw him kick a ball in my life."

"I have, sir. He played soccer in high school, and he can kick a ball a mile. Besides, he's stronger than I am and gets more distance."

"Who's going to hold it?"

"I am."

Ralston glanced at the clock and the timekeeper, and Chip called to the referee for State's last time-out. Now Ralston was on the field and pushing Chip toward the huddle. "Hurry, Hilton. If we get penalized now, we're lost. Go ahead, you make the decision. It's your idea and your choice."

It was then that Chip fully realized the importance of the decision he was about to make. The conference title depended upon this last play of the game. He didn't falter, although his heart was pounding when he entered the huddle. "Hansen will kick," he said quickly. "I'll hold the ball. Fireball, take Hansen's place in the line. Speed, you take Fireball's blocking position. This is it, guys. Seal that line. On four. Let's go!"

Greg's left foot was already out of its shoe, and he tossed it behind him as he took his position for the kick. Every person in the Aggies' Stadium was standing in breathless silence as Chip knelt on the right side of the ball. His mind was racing with lightning speed as he mentally figured the length of the kick. The ball was resting on the thirty-five-yard line; he would place it on the ground seven yards behind the line of scrimmage, and that made forty-two yards. The goal was located on the end-zone line ten yards behind the goal line, and that added up to a fifty-two-yard kick on a wet field!

This kick meant everything to Greg Hansen and the team and the school and the students and Coach Ralston and Mr. and Mrs. Hansen and just about everybody except A & M and their fans, Chip reflected. "Let him make it," he breathed. "Oh, Lord, let him make it!"

Chip's "Hut! Hut! Hut! Hut!" rang out unbelievably clear and loud, and Soapy sent the ball back swift and true as always. Chip plunked it down on the ground and held it steady until he saw Greg's foot fly into and through the ball. Then he closed his eyes and waited in breathless suspense until he heard Soapy's triumphant shout: "ROSE BOWL, HERE WE COME!"

Chip's face reflected his joy. With his eyes still closed, he mouthed a thank-you to God for answering his desperate prayer. How gracious He had been! Chip was deeply touched by that moment—his blessings overflowed.

UNIVERSITY'S six o'clock sportscast was right on time, and Chip leaned back in the overstuffed wing chair and listened to Gee Gee Gray's report on the sports of the day. Gray gave a rundown of the professional football games and then announced that a replay of the final seconds of the State-A & M conference championship game would follow the commercial.

It was warm and pleasant in the Hansen living room, and the appetizing aroma of the dinner that was to follow the replay permeated the room. During the commercial, Chip's thoughts sped back to the events of the past week. Everything had turned out just right. State's football team had completed an undefeated season and won the conference championship. Their bid to the Rose Bowl was sealed and signed. Coach Ralston's father was improving each day, and Curly Ralston had been named NCAA college coach of the year. And, all of Greg Hansen's problems had been solved!

One of the big things to be thankful for were the friendships that had developed after Mr. Hansen's talk with his son. Firsthand evidence of these were right in front of him. Soapy, Biggie, Speed, and Fireball were sprawled comfortably on the living-room floor in front of the TV set, sharing the space with Whip Ward, Flash Hazzard, and Russ Riley. Just across from him, Greg was sitting between his father and mother on the sofa. Chip smiled and winked at them. Not only was everything just right; everything was perfect!

The commercial ended, and then Gee Gee Gray was back on the screen. A second later, the camera shifted to the A & M stadium, the stands overflowing with sixty thousand rain-drenched fans.

"Yes, fans," Gray was saying, "A & M's front four have just dropped Hilton back on the Aggies' thirty-five-yard line for a two-yard loss. Hilton is scrambling to his feet and calls for a time-out. Let's take a look at the scoreboard. . . ."

The camera moved to the scoreboard, and, seeing it for the first time as a spectator, Chip had a good look at it.

| A & M: | 7 | State: | 7 |
| Quarter: | 4 | Time to Play: | 5 Seconds |

The camera swung back to the field and zoomed in on Chip just as he trotted to the sideline for the consultation with Coach Ralston. "You are looking at Hilton now," Gray continued, "number 12, who's talking to Coach Ralston there on the sideline. As you saw on the scoreboard a second ago, fourth down is coming up, and State has the ball on the A & M thirty-five-yard line with only five seconds left to play in this bitter battle for the conference title. Remember now, should this game end in a tie, and it looks that way at this point, a conference championship game ruling requires a sudden-death overtime—

"Hilton is going back on the field. No, he is calling for another time-out, State's last of the game, I believe. Now, he has returned to the sideline and is continuing his discussion with Coach Ralston. Assistant coaches Henry Rockwell, Jim Sullivan, Nick Nelson, and Chet Stewart are standing right behind Ralston.

"Hilton seems to be doing most of the talking. He is undoubtedly discussing State's last-chance play. Will it be a pass or a kick?

"Montague is going out on the field, and now Hilton is following him. Here comes Hazzard out of the game. Montague replaces him for blocking power, I guess. Listen to that hand for Hazzard! The State players are huddled on the A & M forty-five-yard line, ten yards behind the line of scrimmage.

"Hilton kneels at the end of the huddle and gives the play to his teammates. The A & M players are lined up in their 6–3–2 defense, and it's obvious that Coach Pete Riley expects a pass because he has substituted a raft of halfbacks in his lineup.

"State breaks out of the huddle. Hilton is talking to Morris, number 33, the other half of State's crackerjack placekick team. No, hold that! Morris has taken to Finley's blocking position, and Finley is moving into the line to replace Hansen.

"I don't get this at all, but Greg Hansen, number 64, is back in Hilton's kicking position, and Hilton is kneeling to receive the pass from Smith.

"This has to be some kind of a trick play—a fake kick with Hilton passing to Whittemore or Montague, who are at the end positions. Or to Ward or Morris, who are in the blocking positions a yard behind the line of scrimmage.

"Hansen is in position now, and—that's strange! Hilton is lining up seven yards behind the line on the *right* side of the ball. He is facing Whittemore, State's regular tight end.

"Hansen is lining up two yards behind Hilton and to the right as if to try a soccer-style placekick. Hansen is a great blocker and that's probably the reason he's back there. As far as the commentators up here in the TV booth are concerned, no one has even seen or heard of Hansen attempting any kind of a pass or kick before.

"My guess? Hilton is going to pass. He might scramble a bit to give Whittemore or Montague time to get started on a fly, but you can look for a pass with Hansen blocking the first rusher to break through the line.

"The ball is spinning back to Hilton! He is still kneeling! He places the ball on the ground, and Hansen takes three. He's going to kick! I can't believe this! He's going to kick! Hansen boots the ball soccer-style. It's up and it's straight, but I can't tell from here whether it's going to be long enough—

"It is! It is! And it's good!

"The referee has both arms up in the air. The kick is good. It's good, and State has won the game and the conference championship. It's true—the score is up on the big board now. State wins it 10-7!

"What a surprise that was! And how come Hansen hasn't been used for placekicking before? There's only one answer to that: Coach Ralston has been keeping him under wraps for a spot just like this. An unbelievable, impossible, utterly fantastic bit of strategy that has paid off and won State the conference championship and the right to play in the Rose Bowl. What a kick and what a coach and what a storybook finish!"

Chip turned to look at Greg, and the wink they exchanged spelled out more than a thousand words.

The screen now showed one great mass of spectators, State fans for the most part, flowing out of the stands and across the track that circled the gridiron. Overwhelming the stadium police guarding the soggy field, they surrounded the players, cheering them and shouting triumphantly as they patted the Statesmen on their backs and shoulders, tried to shake their hands, or even just touch their heroes.

Chip knew where to look for Greg. He was surrounded by his teammates, who were pushing and punching and banging him on the back and head and roughing him up with hilarious glee. Yes, Chip reflected thankfully, Greg was one of them! He was a true Statesman.

The TV camera zoomed in on Greg just in time to show Fireball and Biggie and Soapy and Speed and Whip and Flash and Russ and one Chip Hilton lifting him to their shoulders and beginning their victory march around the field.

Chip glanced again at his new friend. Greg had an arm around each of his parents' shoulders. His eyes were moist and he was smiling. Mr. Hansen was rubbing his forehead, his hand shielding his eyes. Mrs. Hansen was leaning forward, head bowed, looking steadily at the floor.

Chip guessed he would never forget that family scene, and suddenly there was a tightening in his chest and throat. He swallowed hard and turned to look at the TV set. But for the life of him, he couldn't see the picture on the screen. There was so much to be thankful for! Jesus has a way of making the blessings "pour," too, he reflected.

For a long moment there was a deep silence. Then someone turned off the TV set, and Mr. Hansen leaned forward. "Chip, what were you and Coach Ralston talking about during those two time-outs yesterday afternoon?"

"We were trying to decide whether we should pass or kick," Chip managed to say.

"There was more to it than that, Dad," Greg said. "I'll tell you all about it someday. It's a long story."

"I can wait, I guess," Mr. Hansen said. "Just the same, I'm glad Coach Ralston let you try the kick."

"You can say that again," Chip said quickly.

Greg changed the subject. "Fireball is the greatest fullback I ever saw," he said, leaning forward and slapping Finley on the back. "Imagine, a rushing record of more than three thousand yards in three years of football."

"You're forgetting the Rose Bowl," Soapy said.

"Come off it, you guys," Fireball said. "Anyone could have carried the ball through the holes you fellows were blasting in the line. I'm just glad I got to play with the greatest placekicker in the country."

"I'm glad I got the chance to play beside the greatest center in the country," Hansen said, leaning over and rumpling Soapy's red hair.

"Me too!" Riley added.

"I'm glad a certain blockbusting quarterback turned out to be a great flankerback," Chip said. "And I want to thank him for teaching me how to pass to a tall, skinny end by the name of Hazzard, a player who ran past defensive backs all season as if they were standing still."

"There isn't a quarterback living who can teach you anything about passing," Ward said generously.

"I'm glad I got to know State's football captain," Mrs. Hansen said.

"Me too!" Mr. Hansen said. "And I'm glad I met the greatest cook in the world twenty-five years ago and had enough sense to marry her. Let's eat!"

Afterword

IN 1967 THE MAN EVERYONE CALLED "COACH"
was inducted into the Basketball Hall of Fame as a
contributor to the game. While Clair Bee certainly
deserves recognition as both a coach and contributor to
the game of basketball, the Chip Hilton Sports series
allows my grandfather to continue contributing to the
lives of others even after he is gone. Few basketball
players today are aware of Clair Bee's unmatched winning percentage, but every motion offense and every
pass and cut to the basket retraces the Xs and Os originally sketched by Coach Bee. Few readers today have
seen Chip Hilton's portrait on the orange spine of the
original Chip Hilton series, but with each page turned
they learn the lessons of life and sport originally
taught by my grandfather fifty years ago.

We often bemoan the condition of our surroundings
and even more often wait for someone else to resolve
our problems. The Chip Hilton Sports series teaches us
that everyone, regardless of capacity, has the obliga-
tion and potential to meaningfully contribute to his or
her community. Coach Henry Rockwell of Valley Falls
High School talks to Chip in *Championship Ball* about

having the right spirit to give of himself to his team even when sidelined with injury. Star Athlete Chip Hilton sacrifices his false pride for the benefit of his teammates and becomes team manager Chip Hilton. Clair Bee is the winningest coach in the history of college basketball in terms of his win-loss record, yet he never measured success solely in wins and losses. Clair Bee measured success in how much of himself he gave to his family, friends, readers, and players.

For some, the Chip Hilton Sports series depicts an era gone by that will not return. Let us instead use the Chip Hilton values of respect, dedication, and self-sacrifice as a blueprint to rebuild our families, our communities, and our great nation.

Michael Clair Farley
Grandson

Your Score Card

FIERY FULLBACK

YOUR SCORE CARD

FIERY FULLBACK

CHIP HILTON
MAKES A COMEBACK!

Broadman & Holman Publishers has re-released the popular Chip Hilton Sports Series that first began in 1948 and over an ensuing twenty year period, captivated the hearts and minds of young boys across the nation. The original 23-volume series sold over 2 million copies and is credited by many for starting them on a lifelong love of sports. Today, the long-awaited never-before-published 24th volume, *Fiery Fullback* is available in the updated series and a collector's edition hardcover.

MAKE SURE YOU HAVE ALL OF THE CHIP HILTON BOOKS IN THE SERIES!

Vol. 1 - Touchdown Pass
0-8054-1686-2

Vol. 2 - Championship Ball
0-8054-1815-6

Vol. 3 - Strike Three!
0-8054-1816-4

Vol. 4 - Clutch Hitter!
0-8054-1817-2

Vol. 5 - A Pass and a Prayer
0-8054-1987-X

Vol. 6 - Hoop Crazy
0-8054-1988-8

Vol. 7 - Pitchers' Duel
0-8054-1989-6

Vol. 8 - Dugout Jinx
0-8054-1990-X

Vol. 9 - Freshman Quarterback
0-8054-1991-8

Vol. 10 - Backboard Fever
0-8054-1992-6

Vol. 11 - Fence Busters
0-8054-1993-4

Vol. 12 - Ten Seconds to Play!
0-8054-1994-2

Vol. 13 - Fourth Down Showdown
0-8054-2092-4

Vol. 14 - Tournament Crisis
0-8054-2093-2

Vol. 15 - Hardcourt Upset
0-8054-2094-0

Vol. 16- Pay-Off Pitch
0-8054-2095-9

Vol. 17 - No-Hitter
0-8054-2096-7

Vol. 18 - Triple-Threat Trouble
0-8054-2097-5

Vol. 19 - Backcourt Ace
0-8054-2098-3

Vol. 20- Buzzer Basket
0-8054-2099-1

Vol. 21- Comeback Cagers
0-8054-2100-9

Vol. 22 Home Run Feud
0-8054-2124-6

Vol.- 23 Hungry Hurler
0-8054-2125-4

Vol.- 24 Fiery Fullback
0-8054-2395-8

Vol.- 24 Fiery Fullback
Collectors Edition
0-8054-2418-0

VISIT WWW.CHIPHILTON.COM FOR MORE DETAILS!

About the Author

CLAIR BEE, who coached football, baseball, and basketball at the collegiate level, is considered one of the greatest basketball coaches of all time—both collegiate and professional. His winning percentage, 82.6, ranks first overall among major college coaches, past or present. His name lives on forever in numerous halls of fame. The Coach Clair Bee and Chip Hilton awards are presented annually at the Basketball Hall of Fame, honoring NCAA Division 1 college coaches and players for their commitment to education, personal character, and service to others on and off the court. Coach Clair Bee is the author of the twenty-four-volume, best-selling Chip Hilton Sports series, which has influenced many sports and literary notables, including best-selling author John Grisham.